IT'S JUST ME AND YOU

Ah'Million

Lock Down Publications and Ca$h
Presents

It's Just Me and You

A Novel by *Ah'Million*

Ah'Million

Lock Down Publications
Po Box 944
Stockbridge, Ga 30281

Visit our website @
www.lockdownpublications.com

Lock Down Publications
Like our page on Facebook: Lock Down Publications @
www.facebook.com/lockdownpublications.ldp
Book interior design by: **Shawn Walker**
Edited by: **Mia Rucker**

Stay Connected with Us!

Text **LOCKDOWN** to 22828 to stay up-to-date with new releases, sneak peaks, contests and more…
Thank you.

Submission Guideline.

Submit the first three chapters of your completed manuscript to ldpsubmissions@gmail.com, subject line: Your book's title. The manuscript must be in a .doc file and sent as an attachment. Document should be in Times New Roman, double spaced and in size 12 font. Also, provide your synopsis and full contact information. If sending multiple submissions, they must each be in a separate email.

Have a story but no way to send it electronically? You can still submit to LDP/Ca$h Presents. Send in the first three chapters, written or typed, of your completed manuscript to:

LDP: Submissions Dept
Po Box 944
Stockbridge, Ga 30281

DO NOT send original manuscript. Must be a duplicate.

Provide your synopsis and a cover letter containing your full contact information.

Thanks for considering LDP and Ca$h Presents.

Acknowledgements

First and foremost, all the Glory goes to God. Free King and Del D. Fam, I love y'all. Shout out to Kenny B, my cousin, for doing this time with me, with no complaints. To my people on lock, who have made a bad choice and the system labeled you a bad person, start making the right choices that put you closer to your destiny, instead of the left ones that push you further away. Look more at what you can be grateful for, instead of things to complain about. Sakey, B. Giles, Lu, Tatianna, Lucky, Kib, Pretty P, it's all love on my end. To my fans who enjoy the work I put out, keep riding the wave 'cause I'm not stopping any time soon.

Ah'Million

Prologue

2005

Tears streamed down Danielle's face as she sat uprightly on the edge of Kad's bed. Kad, who was squatted between her legs, reached up and grabbed the sides of her face to cease the chattering of her teeth.

"I can't do this anymore," she sniffed, her large honey colored eyes slowly searching his.

Kad's heart began to beat rapidly as fear seeped in. With a meth addict for a mother and a father he had no knowledge of existing, all he had was his best friend, Bobby, and his girlfriend of merely eleven months, Danielle. Although he and Danielle had only been a pair for almost a year, Kad was mentally and emotionally invested. The thought of losing her sent him into a frenzy.

"Why not? We good, Danielle. I promise." He licked his chapped lips as he waited nervously for a response.

"Kad, I'm due to have this baby in less than forty-eight hours. We're not even prepared. It's not about us anymore. I have to do what's best for the baby."

Kad's lips trembled uncontrollably as he tried gathering the words he would say next. He'd say anything to, at least, buy him some time to change her mind. Tears formed in his eyes.

"You right. Look, if nothing has changed by tomorrow, I'll gladly support whatever decision you make."

Slowly Danielle nodded her head as she used the back of her hand to swap away the tears on her cheeks. Kad stood to his feet, peering down at her. He used his hands to brush away the loose strands that adorned her face. Using his index finger, he tilted her chin until their eyes met.

"I'll be back in an hour. I'm about to go chill with Bobby."

"Okay." Her tone was soft, nearly a whisper.

Danielle lay back on the bed. Kad removed her Old Navy flip flops and massaged her feet. Once Danielle's eyes closed, he pulled the cover up to her neck, and then planted a kiss on her forehead.

Bobby stayed next door to Kad. Kad went inside his closet and knocked on the wall six times. It was a distinctive knock that only he and Bobby knew about. Being that they were so young, and Bobby had caring and attentive parents, He couldn't just simply come and go as he pleased.

Fifteen-year-old Kad, and fourteen year old Bobby, had been friends since the day they were both sent to time out while attending *John W. Ireland* Elementary School. The knock was for emergencies only. Lately, Bobby had been sneaking out more than usual. Being that Danielle was in the last stage of her pregnancy, she had become a bit needy of Things like food and miscellaneous items around the house. He even stole a few hygiene products from his mother to give to Danielle because he knew his best friend simply couldn't provide it.

Bobby jolted upright, hearing the knock in his sleep. His shoes sat on the side of his bed. He slipped on his black joggers and Nike hoodie, and placed his feet inside his shoes. Bobby was always on go. His house was clean as a nursing home, and quiet as a library. He crept down the hall to his parents' room. He eased against the door, placing his ear against it to assure that they were asleep, before returning to his room and creeping out of his window.

Bobby's parents were older. His mother was a stay at home mom. She handled her wifely duties and nothing more. His father did janitorial work at his old elementary school, which resulted in many fights because Bobby was teased a lot. His dad was very strict and attentive. His mother caring and gentle. They didn't have a lot, but they had enough. Bobby never went without a meal, bath, water, or the necessities for school. Most of all, they had each other. They were united in love.

The wintry weather forced Bobby to move like he had fire underneath his feet. The thin Nike hoodie was no match for the freezing temp. Luckily, Kad stayed so close and he was familiar with the route, because there wasn't a glimpse of light anywhere in sight. Bobby let himself inside Kad's place, something he did every time, not wanting to alert Kad's mother with his presence.

Kad's mother, Ms. Christy, sold pussy to nearby dealers, and anyone else who was willing and wanting to buy it, just to secure her next fix. The place was pretty spacious, being that they didn't possess much furniture. The sofa and shelf looked older than Bobby, but seeing that he couldn't help the situation, he refused to speak on it. A foul stench lingered throughout the house. Bobby was starting to think the smell was as permanent as the paint on the walls.

He rushed inside Kad's room, which was located in the back of the apartment. Kad was knelt at the foot of the bed. His fingers were intertwined, and his eyes closed. Sensing Bobby's presence, Kad ended his prayer. Then he slowly stood to his feet. He pecked Danielle's forehead, and then signaled Bobby toward the hallway.

"I got a plan. It's simple, but its adequate." He peered at Bobby through pleading eyes.

Hearing the tone of Kad's voice made Bobby's heartbeat speed up. He had a feeling that tonight's mission would be a little different than the ones before. Bobby and Kad had done tedious things previously, like mob to the nearest convenience store. Kad would steal an item or two, and Bobby would purchase something small so they wouldn't appear as thieves.

"What's the plan? Whatever it is, we have to hurry up and do it, then get back. Lately, my dad been checking on me at odd times of the night 'cause he caught me playing the game at 3am last week."

"We going to hit the car wash," Kad stated seriously.

Bobby's eyes widened in bewilderment. He wasn't sure if he'd heard him right. "What you mean hit the car wash?"

"Look, it's not what you think. I heard Mo and Youngsta talking about it. They did it two weeks ago and got four hundred dollars in quarters and cash," Kad admitted, hoping to convince Bobby.

"But I don't need no bread, Kad. I'm good."

Kad's shoulders sunk in defeat. "Danielle is saying-"

"Say less," Bobby stated. He may have not been hurting for money, but he knew his boy's situation. There was no need to explain what was clearly overstood.

"I know where they keep the tool at."

Kad and Bobby walked side by side through the apartment complex.

"It's over there." Kad pointed to the dumpster. The boys jogged to the dumpster, easily spotting the crowbar propped against the wooden fence.

"Let's make this quick."

***

The traffic along the main strip caused Bobby's heart to beat thunderously inside his chest.

"Bruh, it's too open. Are you sure about this?" Bobby's veins protruded from his neck as he swung his hands wildly.

Kad grabbed Bobby by the shoulders peering directly into his eyes. "I need this, Bobby. Danielle drops any day now. She's just a kid. We're kids. We don't have milk, clothes, not even soap to bathe with." Kad gritted his teeth, the crocodile tears in no rush to escape.

"But what about the hospital? Won't they give y'all the bare minimum before she leaves?" Bobby bargained. He wanted to do anything but what they were about to do.

"We not going to the hospital. We can't! Danielle is having the baby right at home. Ms. Lula already agreed to help us."

Bobby sighed deeply, brushing his waves with his sweaty palms. "Alright, come on."

Both boys emerged from the shadows. Traffic was still light, but Kad wasted no time removing the crowbar from the book bag.

"I just need you to give me eyes," Kad mumbled as he approached the nearest machine. He lifted the crowbar slid it in between the master lock and forcefully yanked downward.

Clack!

The lock snapped open and collided onto the concrete. Kad opened the door on the machine and gathered the cash and coins.

"I'll handle that, Kad, go to the next one."

Kad sped from the machine and headed towards the next one.

Bobby spun around in terror. "Hey, you hear that?"

Kad was opening the door on the machine. He hadn't heard a word Bobby said. "I need the backpack, Bobby," Kad whispered loudly.

Bobby rushed towards him. His eyes were wide as golf balls. "Kad! Do you hear that?"

Finally, Kad paused. The only thing that moved was his chest as it heaved. The sirens could be heard from a distance, but there was no denying what the sound was.

"We gotta go!" Bobby retreated slowly.

Kad swiftly gathered the rest of the coins.

The sirens grew louder.

"Kad, come on!"

The desperation in Bobby's voice snapped Kad out of his trance, forcing him to think rationally. Kad scrambled to his feet and take off in the direction they had come. Bobby was already a few feet ahead of him. The boys hopped the four-foot fence and landed in the neighborhood park. It had rained the night before, forcing the boys to tread through the mud. The sirens were so loud you would've thought the police were right behind them, but as Kad peered over his shoulder, there wasn't anyone in sight.

Midway through the park, Kad yelled, "Hold up! Hold up!"

Bobby turned around and checked things out before his legs stopped moving.

"What we stopping for?" Bobby asked, panting for breath.

"We need to split up, Bobby," Kad suggested. He was hunched over with his hands resting on top of his knees.

"Hell no, that's dumb. We need to keep moving."

"Bobby, if both of us get spotted together, and I have this damn backpack on, it's a dead giveaway."

Bobby smacked his lips in frustration. "Put the money in your pocket and toss that tool and backpack in the bushes."

"Here." Kad stretched his closed fist full of bills toward Bobby.

"Man, keep that. That's for your seed. I just tagged along 'cause you didn't want to come alone." His hasty speech and swift eye movement certainly indicated that he was spooked. "Come on. We got to move." Urgency laced his words.

Kad reached out and pulled his best friend into a hug.

"I'll see you back at the crib," Kad managed before jogging away from Bobby.

Headed in two different directions, the boys sprinted into darkness with high hope of making it back home. The desire to make it back was no greater for one than the other. Kad had to make it back because, if not, he'd surely lose the love of his life and the seed growing inside of her. Bobby had to, as well, because if he was caught for some reason, he would disappoint his parents, and his father would beat him like a drum.

Bobby ran until his chest began to tighten. He slowed and peered over his shoulder at Kad, whose pace had slowed as well. Bobby stepped onto the sidewalk, slightly blending in with the branches and leaves that hung from the huge trees that set in the center of the yard. For a moment, time slowed. The police cruiser slowed before halting at the stop sign, which was merely a few feet away from Kad, but a considerable distance from Bobby.

Bobby's breathing ceased as he quickly leaned up against the fence. Kad, whose back was to him, was unaware of the police behind him.

"Kad!" Bobby yelled with every ounce of strength and breath in his body. He stepped away from the fence.

Kad froze. Then, suddenly, the police cruiser's lights came on and it swiftly swerved left, in Kad's direction. Kad ran a *slant* so cold that he looked like a baby Terrell Owens. A slant is a route run by the wide receiver when he runs straight ahead for a five to ten yards, then bears swiftly to the left or right. Once Kad made the swift left, he ended up making a complete circle, heading in Bobby's direction.

The police cruiser made an illegal U-turn on the narrow street.

As Kad grew closer, Bobby peered around, terror stricken, indecisive about his next move. He peered inside the yard through the metal fence. He rushed around the fence and into the yard, which belonged to someone he had no knowledge of, and hid behind the massive oak tree. He spotted Kad, as he dashed into the park. Although Bobby had to squint just to see, he was able to catch Kad scooting underneath the merry-go-round.

Another police cruiser pulled up. Bobby was so shaken up that he had literally stopped breathing to prevent urinating on himself. He could only imagine how Kad felt.

By now, both policemen were searching around the park, guns drawn, along with a flashlight. Kad lay underneath the merry-go-round, shaking like a stripper. He held on to the thick metal to cease the quivering, but it didn't work. Once they spotted him, his fate would be sealed as soon as they found the ridiculous amount of change in his pocket.

The sound of footsteps approaching forced Kad to shut his eyes and clench his butt cheeks, in hopes to appear invisible.

"Call for backup and tell em' to bring the dogs. I saw this motherfucker with my own eyes."

Kad gritted his teeth in anger. They would surely find him now.

Bobby couldn't slow the pace of his heart after hearing the officer speak into his radio. He lowered his head in defeat. Then he placed his thumb and index finger over his lids, while pondering the inevitable. He wished he would've just asked his father for help, instead of taking matters into his own hands. The money probably wouldn't have been as quick and easy, but eventually they would've gotten it, and no consequences would've come with it. Bobby sighed deeply. He leaped from around the tree.

"I'm right here," he yelled trying to appear strong on wobbly knees.

"Get down on the ground! Get down," the officers yelled as they both swarmed Bobby, guns high.

Bobby slowly dropped to one knee, the other one followed.

The headlights on the cruiser shined directly on Kad. If the men would've moved further back, they would've been able to spot him.

Kad and Bobby locked eyes as the policeman placed the cuffs around his wrists. The dip in his brows and stream of tears displayed Kad's feelings inwardly as he peered at his best friend. Bobby shrugged, then lowered his head, breaking the glare.

"Where's the money?"

"I ditched it down the street by the dumpster," Bobby lied to prevent them for searching the park.

"Don't be shitting me! If you are, that's another charge," the officer screamed, pointing his finger at Bobby's face.

Bobby nodded his head slowly in agreement.

"Let's move."

Chapter 1
Kad 2021

"You set and ready, baby girl?" Kad asked his daughter, Jewel, peering cheerfully inside her room.

She smacked her lips. "Yeah, I guess so."

He eased inside and sat on the edge of her bed. "Look, I know you miss her. I do too, but you have to be strong." He pulled the covers up to her neck.

"I know, dad, but I miss her so much," Jewel expressed as tears filled her eyes.

Danielle, the mother of his child and beat of his heart, had passed away nearly a year ago due to breast cancer. He peered immensely into his daughter's eyes, hoping she'd cheer up before he broke down. Kad had loved Danielle more than life itself. So, to lose her was hazardous to his health. Using his thumb to swipe away the tear from Jewel's cheek, sadness consumed him because of his lack of consolation.

"Your mother wouldn't want to see you down. You have to stay focused so you can excel and help prevent other women from losing their life to the fatal disease."

Since losing Danielle, Jewel had her mind set on being an oncologist. She planned to help women not just fight, but conquer, the deadly disease that brought her so much pain and strife.

"Okay, dad, you right," she spoke through sniffles, sighing deeply in surrender.

"I love you." Kad placed a kiss on her forehead.

"I love you, too."

Jewel was starting her senior year of high school tomorrow and Kad wasn't the least excited. Like most parents, he wished his baby girl could stay young forever. So much for wishful thinking. After easing her door closed, he lowered his head, squeezing the bridge of his nose as he forced his eyes shut. He deeply sighed before walking away. His issues were immutable.

Kad headed down the stairway, then into the kitchen. He needed something brown and strong to ease his mind. Spotting the bottle of Hennessey made his mouth water, yet he chose the VSOP instead. He poured the liquid into a short glass, filling it to the rim before tossing it back. He did it again, then again. Calmly, he dragged himself to the living room, and stretched out on the sofa. He closed his eyes and, shortly after, drifted off into a deep sleep.

The sound of Kad's phone ringing interrupted his sleep. He peered around, somewhat confused, forgetting that he passed out on the sofa, instead of his bed.

Hello?" Kad answered groggily.

"Mr. McVale?" Hearing the urgency in his secretary's tone, he jolted forward.

"Yes, I'm here."

"Mr. Dunbar just called to reschedule the meeting." She paused. "He'll be here in an hour."

Coupled with frustration was anger that penetrated his body. Today was Jewel's first day of school. He didn't want to miss it.

"Did he say why he rescheduled?" Kad questioned in confusion.

"He mentioned another important meeting he has to attend."

"Damn! Let me call you back."

At thirty-one, life couldn't get any better for Kad, financially. He wasn't just the CEO of his record label, *New Money Ent*. He was also the founder of the non-profit organization *Weallin*, which was as lucrative as the label. For years, he held the loyalty Bobby had shown him on that night close to his heart. Being that he could never even the score and grant him the time he lost, he tried doing so in different areas. After Bobby was released from prison in 2015, Kad blessed him, making Bobby the C.O.O. of both of his businesses. He and Bobby both shared a passion for music, fear of imprisonment, and a desire for wealth. So everything worked out fine, or so Kad believed.

Mr. Dunbar was a generous investor that Kad had been waiting weeks to meet with. Missing this opportunity wasn't an option.

Kad called Bobby to fill him in on what was happening.

"This dude done rescheduled the meeting," Kad yelled in frustration.

"Rescheduled? For when?"

"It's for today, in an hour. I promised Jewel I'd take her to school." The shit vexed Kad's spirit just thinking about it.

"Go ahead and take her. I'll fill in for you at the meeting."

Bobby knew the importance of the meeting, and so did Kad. That's why he chose to go instead. Bobby was as familiar with the meeting process as Kad, but Bobby lacked people skills.

"I'll just get Bey to take her for me." Bey was Kad's older sister. They were not as close as most siblings, but they were close enough.

"Good luck with that," Bobby commented.

Kad sighed in surrender.

"I'll take her, and you take care of the meeting. I'll swing by the office, once I drop her off," Bobby suggested.

"Preciate it, I'll let her know you're coming," Kad reluctantly replied.

"Bet. Give me twenty minutes."

Click

"Jewel!" He rushed down the hall, fastening the buttons on his shirt.

"Baby." Kad halted once Jewel's door swung open.

"Huh?" she answered, batting her lashes.

He gritted his teeth to subdue his anger. Jewel was as beautiful as her mother. The thought of men salivating over his daughter left a bad taste in his mouth. Her brown skin was free of blemishes, with a natural and subtle glow. Her makeup was applied flawlessly, enhancing her natural beauty, but concealing her youth.

Kad lowered his head as he gripped his lips. "Aye, Jewel, take that eye shadow stuff off. You don't need all that." A part of him hated that he was so overprotective. He wanted badly for Jewel to express herself in more ways than one and do whatever brought joy and peace into her weighty life, but the fatherly side always exceeded.

"But, dad, all my friends are wearing it," Jewel whined.

"I don't give a damn, you're seventeen."

Jewel turned around. She sat on the edge of her bed with her arms folded at her chest.

Kad halted, seeing her upset. But if she thought he was going to conform to the "New Society," she had another thing coming. "Hey, I have a very important meeting to attend. I'll make it up to you later. Bobby will be here shortly to pick you up."

Chapter 2
Jewel

The mentioning of Bobby's name made Jewel's heart flutter. Despite the emotions her father stirred, Bobby's effect was unfailing, and he didn't even know it. But knowing that Bobby was on his way, swelled her irritation. She couldn't believe how irrational her father was being on her first day of school. It was bad enough he was putting work before her... again.

Tears fell down her face. She quickly patted her cheeks dry before the salty liquid ruined her beat. Just as he requested, she took a Q-tip and carefully removed the eye shadow, without touching her mink lashes. The twenty-four-carat gold matched her skin tone perfectly, but since it was too much for Kad, she applied a hazel nut color instead that practically matched her skin tone.

Jewel spun around on the stool in the direction of the window. The sound of bass and loud music seemed to have been magnified.

Bobby. Shit. She rushed and peered out of the blinds, only to confirm her assumption. Her hands shook nervously as she prepped for her departure. She slung her Fendi bag over her shoulder and rushed out of the bedroom. Spotting the money on the counter, she slid it into her cargo shorts and jogged out the front door.

Her stomach started doing summersaults the closer she got to his truck. "Hey, Bobby." Jewel never lifted her head as she climbed inside of his truck. His presence was intimidating and inflexible, forcing her to cower in his company.

He simply greeted her with a head nod as he continued to bob his head to the Lil Baby lyrics. He never looked at her longer than a second to admire her beauty, like she hoped he would. Although Bobby was just a year younger than her father, he looked and dressed like the guys ten years his junior. Prison had preserved him. Jewel was unsure of the exact amount of time he served, but she was certain he did some.

"Bobby?" She peered up. He obviously didn't hear her. He didn't flinch or peer in her direction. "Bobby!" She waited.

Jewel deeply sighed. She was going to have to touch him to get his attention. Her heart beat rapidly. She didn't want to. Nervous was an understatement. After a few short breaths she mustered up enough courage. She reached out and placed her freshly manicured hands on his shoulder.

Bobby's head snapped quickly in her direction. He lowered the volume on the music.

"What's up?"

"Can you please stop by Aunt Bey house and pick up Myesha?"

He never took his eyes off the road. "Yeah, where she stay?" His deep raspy voice resembled the rapper Pop Smoke. Just looking at him made

Jewel clench her thighs to subdue the tingling in her kitty. "Buckner Village."

Bobby turned the volume up. Even if she had something else to say, it didn't matter.

Since knowing him, he had always been a man of few words. Although he came around often, getting close to him was impossible, so it seemed. Ever since she could remember, she'd had a crush on him. Of course, he paid her no attention. He'd been friendly and polite whenever he would visit, but she eventually realized that was done out of respect. His swag screamed D-boy, but drugs wasn't his hustle. All Bobby's money was legitimate.

Afraid to boldly look in his direction, Jewel cut her eyes at Bobby. His caramel skin was smooth, with the exception of a scar above his brow. His beard was full but trimmed low. It was always lined up to perfection. He turned the volume down.

"Hey, that's Bey daughter?" he asked, seemingly confused. He leaned forward as he drove through the entryway.

Myesha stood beside the rent office, speaking aggressively into her phone. The mug on her face vanished once she spotted Bobby's Escalade truck. Jewel spotted Bobby's lip curl upward at the sight of Myesha.

"Aunt Bey's car is in the shop, so she wasn't able to drop her off at school," Jewel spoke, while pretending to examine her nails.

Bobby slowly nodded in agreement. Just last year, she was attending a private school for the talented and gifted. After Danielle, passed things changed. Not only did Jewel's world spiral out of control, but so did her grades. Failure to maintain academically, she was forced out.

"Cool," he agreed, turning the volume up.

Come and put that pussy on me/Don't be runnin' from me/If I like it, I spend money on it/Get whatever from me.

Jewel turned around in the seat and smiled at her cousin. Myesha and Jewel's bond had strengthened since Danielle's death. Danielle didn't really like Jewel hanging around at her cousin's house because she was aware of and displeased with Bey's character. Jewel eyed Myesha in admiration. Her bold eye shadow was perfectly blended, complementing the shape of her bedroom eyes. The highlight against her dark skin made her look exotic.

Approaching the school, which she had heard so many rumors about, Jewel became nervous. But she was ready to see what all the Hype was about. As soon as Bobby's truck rolled to a stop, both of them hung their designer masks on their ears and climbed out the truck.

"Aye, we here, bitch," Myesha yelled in her high pitch voice.

Jewel poked her head inside the truck before shutting it.

"Thanks, Bobby." She smiled, hoping he'd acknowledge her long enough to revel in her beauty. He reached inside his pocket, peeled a hundred-dollar bill from the wad of money, and passed it to her.

"Be good," he mumbled.

If she hadn't been anticipating his response, she would've missed it. She peered at the money perplexed.

"My dad left me money this morning."

He peered into her direction for merely a second, long enough for her to catch a glimpse of his honey colored eyes.

"Well now you have more." He tore his eyes from her amid his response.

Jewel caught the hint and closed the door to his truck close.

"Bye, Bobby!" Myesha hollered from the curb. She waved seductively as she bounced lightly on her tip toes, making her breast jiggle.

Paying her no mind, Bobby sped off.

"That nigga is mean as fuck, but he look so good." "Come on, cousin," Myesha announced as she led the way into Skyline High.

Chapter 3
Bobby

"Hey Lady," Bobby greeted his grandmother as he stepped through the foyer of her three-bedroom house.

"Hey, suga, come give me some love. I missed you yesterday." She stretched out her arms as she sat on the love seat.

Scriptures and Christian art adorned the walls. Bobby's grandmother had been staying in the same house before his imprisonment. A year after his release, he renovated the whole place. He hugged her large frame tightly, planting a kiss on her cheek.

"You haven't missed a day since you got out." She peered at him over her glasses.

Bobby sighed deeply. He sat the chicken on the table in front of her, then flopped down on the sofa.

"I know, big momma, I had got *real* busy. I won't do it again. I promise."

Bobby sprinted to the kitchen and grabbed a plate off the cabinet. He returned, opened the box of chicken, and placed all the food on the plate. Williams Chicken was her favorite.

She picked up the plate with both hands. Her hands shook uncontrollably. It was a side effect from the medication she was taking. Bobby's grandmother was a diabetic. She ate healthy six days out of a week. But on Mondays, Bobby gave her a pass, and gave her the option to eat whatever her stomach desired. She placed the plate inside her lap and went to work.

Lost in his own thoughts, Bobby's eyes landed on a family picture of him with his mother and father. A lonely tear slid down his cheek. He swiped it swiftly with the back of his hand before his grandmother noticed. Seconds passed.

"I miss him, too," she spoke in between chewing her food.

Bobby peered at her, perplexed. His eyebrows dipped in confusion. He lightly chuckled, after realizing she must've seen the tear. He always thought his grandmother had eyes at the back of her head. Many times, she proved his silly theory to be accurate.

"I just. Never mind." During the ten-year stint Bobby spent in prison, the isolation had turned him into a very secretive person. He put a lid on his emotions and stored them inside. Inwardly, he was a pantry.

"Talk to me, baby. You know you can talk to big momma about anything," she assured, pushing her glasses closer to her eyes.

"I miss him, granny. I still today harbor guilt because I wasn't here with him when he took his last breath. He was always there for me." Bobby pointed to his chest.

Big momma was the only one with a key to the pantry. She was practically the only family he had left.

After being jailed for the theft at the car wash, Bobby was sentenced to five years in TYC, a prison for youth. After four years of being incarcerated, Bobby was informed of his father's illness. The colon cancer enveloped him quickly, ending his life at the age of forty-one. The death of the man he'd idolized since birth caused him to lash out viciously. Mentally deranged, and unaware of the weight of his actions, he possessed no concern for the unforeseen consequences.

A result of his savagery was not only a new charge, but a new sentence of five years that he'd have to complete as well. The female CO he brutally beat during one of his tantrums had to be hospitalized after his attack. So many nights after that night, he wanted to give up, in hopes of ending up in the same place as his father, but he knew things weren't so simple. The only light during those dark days was visitation from his mother.

One day, a visit with his mother changed Bobby's insight and perception on life altogether. Since that day, he never acted out or did anything that would jeopardize his release date. He still could effortlessly visualize the moment like it was yesterday. Her small hands clasped tightly over his.

"Listen to me, son," her lips quivered as she spoke. "I need you to do whatever it is that you have to do so that you can make it home to me." She paused. "I'm trying to hold on 'til you get here. I'm trying." Tears formed in her eyes. She lowered her head.

Bobby squinted at her from across the table, panicky and startled. "Ma?" he questioned.

She lifted her head. Tears flowed down her cheeks. "Son, honestly, I died years ago with your father. The only thing that gives me life is the possibility of reuniting with you. I don't know how much longer I can fight, but I need you to fight this with me 'cause you all I got."

Bobby made his mother a promise that day that he never broke, and neither did she. She fought a good fight.

However, shortly after he was released, she died of a broken heart, or so he assumed, since the doctors never discovered her cause of death. It was probably because his mother and father had been together since the age of fifteen, and married fresh out of high school. Even her love for her only son wasn't adequate enough to balance it all out.

"Bobby, you have to let go and let God," Big Momma said, bringing him out of his trance. "That happened years ago. You been out of that place for seven years, and you still haven't made me any grandchildren." She licked the grease from her fingers.

Women were the furthest thing from his mind, especially children. There was no way he would risk losing his own seed. Women were simply used for casual sex. His prison stint helped him become more accustomed to isolation. He wasn't just used to it, but he grew fond of it, as well. The pain from the loss of his parents numbed him, transforming him into a being that held little to no emotion. With women, he'd mastered the art of *detachment*.

"There you go, lady. Don't start." He lightly chuckled.

He retrieved the dirty plate from her lap and washed it, along with the others. He cleaned anything else he considered to be out of place before joining her in the living room. They conversed for another hour or so before Bobby said his goodbyes.

Outside of the non-profit organization and record label, Bobby had another hustle. Instead of flipping packs, he flipped houses. He drove at a snail's pace down the street in which his house was located. Surveying the neighborhood, everything seemed normal, except the light traffic across the street from the house he owned.

A group of young dudes were huddled up in front of a garage, smoking and capping. Their laughter could be heard over Bobby's loud music. He sneered at their foolishness. Bobby eased further down to a stopping point alongside the curb.

Spotting the unfamiliar truck across the street, the young men squinted their eyes, frowning in his direction.

Bobby hopped out.

They began to whisper to one another.

Bobby peered in their direction, peeping the sudden silence. Even if he tried to make out what they were saying, it would've been impossible. He didn't even bother to kill the engine. Bobby wasn't a dealer, nor was he in the mix, but he was inferior to no one. He didn't sag his Amiri's or snap selfies with Draco's, nor did he mistreat people and act uncivilized just because he had the money, which brings power to do so.

He climbed the porch stairs and peered through the windows. He then jerked the door knob a few times to assure it was still secure, before walking away. Bobby glared at the young men, who were still watching him. He nodded, hoping they'd speak instead, but they returned the gesture. He hopped back in his ride and headed towards the office he and Kad shared.

Chapter 4
Blotchy

Blunts of loud were in rotation inside of the spacious smoke shop. A group of men huddled up in a circle were aggressively exchanging words and shooting dice. Some kneeled, some stood. Blotchy hovered over the mayhem, standing only a few feet away. Physically, he was in the smoke shop, but mentally, he was at the studio. He walked behind the counter and peered out of the window. In a few minutes, school would be letting out, and young customers would file in.

"Blotchy, give me another hunnid," Big Dooski yelled over his shoulder. Urgency laced his words, instantly snapping Blotchy out of his trance.

Confusion sketched his face. "This nigga done hit you again?" Bobby stepped from around the counter, easing closer to the action. He dug around in his pocket. "It ain't no pressure on no bread." He handed Big Dooski the hundred-dollar bill. "Watch out, Dooski, let me fade em' real quick."

Big Dooski sighed deeply before scooting to the side. He and Blotchy had been friends for years.

"What it's hittin' fo'?" Blotchy asked the light skinned dude as he squatted down in front of him. The men locked eyes for seemingly minutes before another word was spoken.

"Shoot ten, bet ten."

Both men tossed their money in the pot. The dude rolled an eight.

"Twenty, I hit eight." He peered up at Blotchy with the dub in his hand.

"Nigga, I roll my weed in dubs. Put fifty on it." Blotchy glared at him boldly, then tossed a fifty in the center of the floor.

"Bruh, you disrespectful, handling me like I'm some type of goofy ass nigga. Make it a hunnid." The side of his lip curled upward, exposing the diamonds in his mouth.

"Shoot," Blotchy urged, adding fifty more dollars to the pot.

He shook the dice. The dice hit the floor. Everyone scanned them quickly. One landed on a six, the other a two. He hit his point.

"Give me my money!" The light skinned dude stood to his feet. He was elated. Bending at the waist, he snatched his money off the floor. He stepped around the other man, who was knelt down, waiting to roll the dice.

Shame pervaded Blotchy, even though he tried his best to conceal it. "Aye, where you going, bruh? I'm not done. I can do this all day," Blotchy capped, while thumbing through the crisp bills in his hand.

The dude turned completely around.   "I'm sure you can, but, bruh, I'm done. I'm about to go fuck my bitch."

The smirk on his face made Blotchy's blood boil. He stood to his feet, with squinted eyes and flared nostrils. "So you just gon' take my shit? Fuck that. Me and my nigga shit, and leave?"

The room went silent. The dude remained speechless as he stood there with his hands buried in his pockets, obviously unbothered. Blotchy stepped closer.

"Leave that shit Alone, Blotchy. Let him have them dollars," Big Dooski hollered.

Truthfully, Blotchy didn't need a label. But he wanted to be a part of one. However, his street involvement was a hindrance. Big Dooski's words made Blotchy reconsider what he was about to do. His shoulders slumped in surrender. He had come to his senses.

"*Tuh.*" The light skinned dude peered at Blotchy courageously, then turned to walk away.

Appalled by his level of disrespect, Blotchy swiftly struck him on the side of his head, close to his temple. The dude stumbled. Blotchy rushed him, raining blow after blow on his face and the top of his head. He dropped to his knees.

"Get up! I'm gon' let your bitch ass get up," he yelled. Blotchy hovered over him.

Big Dooski rushed from the rear of the store. He stood in between Blotchy and the dude, who was struggling to stand.

"That's enough, B. Just chill."

Slowly the dude stood to his feet. He appeared to be in and out of consciousness.

"Watch out," Blotchy ordered, pushing past his friend.

The dude shook it off and planted his feet. His stance was spineless and sloppy as he removed the blood that constantly dripped down his eye from the gash above his brow.

Blotchy threw an uppercut, in an attempt to finish him. Shockingly, he blocked it.

The dude rushed Blotchy with a combination of his own. He threw up his hands to block the punches, but he wasn't quick enough to block the first two or three. The blows stung Blotchy, but the taste of blood angered him. He rushed the guy, swiftly attacking his mid-section. But this time when he dropped to his knees, Blotchy hit him with a right hook that rocked him to sleep.

However, that wasn't enough. He climbed on top of him and punched him ceaselessly until he felt hands tugging at his shirt and dragging him away.

After returning to his senses, Blotchy headed to the rear of the store to rinse his hands of the blood that stained them. He took a few minutes to gather his thoughts before returning to the chaos. However, it wasn't as chaotic as he thought it'd be. As soon as he emerged from the restroom, Big Dooski was heading toward him.

"I paid one of them young niggas to drop him off in front of his apartment."

"Bet."

The bell sounded, snatching both of their attention.

Chapter 5
Myesha

Jewel and Myesha entered the smoke shop down the street from their school. Myesha had worn khaki leggings instead of actual uniform pants that she made certain to pull up, upon entering the store. Exposing her camel toe, she strutted inside. It was something a little different about today, but she didn't speak on it. Since Kad was running a little late, the girls figured they'd have themselves some fun while waiting.

"Oooh, bitch, there go Blotchy," Myesha mumbled nudging Jewel's side.

She knew the store belonged to Blotchy. She had been to the store a thousand times but only saw him once. Seeing him emerge from the back was so shocking.

Jewel gazed at the handsome rap star admiringly.

"It's a whole lot of money in this motherfucka!" Myesha chanted as she locked eyes with the guy standing next to Blotchy.

He was taller and chubbier. Myesha found him strikingly handsome. The attraction must've been mutual. He paused, reveling in her beauty, perhaps her camel toe, too. He leaned against the counter a few feet away from her. Myesha simply smiled because her words were caught in her throat. Using his index finger and thumb he pinched the tip of his dick.

"What's up? What y'all got going on?" He asked.

Myesha, who was still staring down at his pants, thought, "Damn, if his dick hangs that low on soft, I can only imagine it on hard."

"Smoke and hangout."

"Her dad on his way to pick her up, so whatever we decide, it won't last long."

His size may have been intimidating, but his features were harmless and magnetic. He was black as oil, with eyes the color of cinnamon. His beard was shiny and kempt, complimenting his full pouty lips.

"Oh, how old are you, schoolgirl?"

"Old enough."

He chuckled at her feistiness, placing his fist in front of his mouth. He'd done it more than once, forcing Myesha to believe his teeth were jacked.

"Ok, Ms. Grown ass. I'll see how grown you is. Let me get your number." He palmed the top of his head.

"Waves on swim so they hate on him," she jokingly sang the Nicki Minaj lyrics.

"Girl, give me the number."

They exchanged phones and inserted their information.

"Okay, Ms. Myesha," he recited.

"Big Dooski? What kind of name is-"

"I don't give a fuck, you young ass bitch!"

Myesha turned around at the sound of screaming. Blotchy was yelling at Jewel, pointing towards the door.

Jewel, being the timid and sheepish girl Myesha had always known her to be, stayed silent, then lowered her head.

"Like your shit made of gold. Get the fuck on," he spoke harshly, with so much aggression that his veins protruded from his neck. Jewel took off and ran out of the store. She had never felt so humiliated.

"Fuck you and your store," Myesha told Blotchy before running after Jewel.

***

"Hey Momma," Myesha said dryly. She had grown tired of staying in the small, rundown apartment with her mother.

"Hey," Bey answered back with a bite.

"Hey, Niecy Pooh!"

Jewel dropped her bag on the couch and shared a hug with her aunt.

Myesha watched her mother from a distance, sneering at her fraudulence. Bey didn't love Jewel simply because she was her niece. She loved her because she was beneficial. Jewel either had the drugs or the money to buy it. One thing her mother couldn't stand was a broad with no money. Her favorite line was "As long as you got a pussy, you should never be broke." Her golden rule did not exclude here children, Myesha, Bianca, and Brandi. Listed from the youngest to the oldest, they'd all had it rough living under their mother's rules. Bianca and Brandi moved out last year. Myesha was saving up so she could do the same.

"Where that good at?" Bey asked, exposing her gold teeth.

There were two things she enjoyed the most, talking shit and smoking weed.

Jewel swiftly cut her eyes in Myesha's direction, catching her roll her eyes. She knew how Myesha felt about her mother, but she simply couldn't relate, being that Bey was good to her. Myesha walked past her mother and cousin, mumbling obscenities under her breath.

"What you say, bitch?" Bey asked simultaneously as her head swiveled in Myesha's direction.

"Nothing, momma, dang." Lowering her head, she headed towards her room.

Bey liked to go on and on. She figured she'd disappear in hopes she'd switch the topic.

Bey eyed her daringly. "That's what I thought. You need to be trying to secure a bag because your time ticking, bitch. If you ain't got no funds to contribute to next month's rent, you getting up out of here!" She flopped down on the sofa.

"Here, Aunty." Jewel handed her the small bag of loud.

Upon entering, Myesha convinced Jewel to separate two grams from the pack, and stash the rest, knowing Bey would smoke whatever they possessed. Jewel didn't mind smoking all her weed with Aunt Bey. They were permitted to smoke freely. No consequences. Free of worries and fear of being caught. Myesha, on the other hand, would rather smoke uncomfortably than to be around her mother.

"Damn, this all y'all heffas got?" Bey complained. "Let me go get my papers." She walked to the rear of the house.

Myesha returned looking pissy. "As soon as we smoke this joint, we out," she spat, with her arms crossed over her chest.

Her mother strolled into the living room with her container of papers and a shoebox lid. It wasn't long before smoke and laughter filled the small room.

"When that nigga got loud with you, niece, you should've said, *Fuck you shrimp dick!*"

Jewel erupted in laughter. She thought her Aunt Bey was the funniest woman in the world. She looked forward to hearing the raw and ratchet shit that poured from her mouth.

A knock at the door grabbed all of their attention. Bey sneered at the door in confusion. She jumped to her feet and stormed towards it. She flung the door open.

"Oh, hey, baby!"

A tall dude stood at the entryway. Myesha peered over her shoulder and vanished, once she spotted his familiar face. He appeared ten to twelve years older than Bey, with a jagged posture. Jewel assumed he was disabled. She peered back at Myesha for confirmation, but the spot that Myesha once occupied was now empty. She shrugged and continued to hit the weed.

"Hey, y'all, I don't know where y'all going, but y'all got to get the hell out of here! My man is here."

Jewel peered back at Bey jokingly. She brushed it off, turning back around.

Myesha appeared in front of her. "Bruh, she's serious," she announced dryly. Her face was stern, humorless. She appeared familiar with the routine.

Jewel, on the other hand, was stunned. "Oh, I'm sorry, Aunty. I thought you was just playing," she said timidly, struggling to quickly gather her things.

"Nah, Niecy Pooh, I don't play about my man. It's nothing against you, but I be damn if I let one of these young ho's take him from me."

A nervous chuckle escaped Jewels lips as she made her exit. Shame and hatred filled Myesha's eyes as she tried to appear unbothered.

Although, Jewel knew inwardly it pained her deeply to know her own mother didn't trust her. "Come on. When we get here don't mention anything to my dad about what just happened."

Myesha nodded in agreement. The girls smoked blunt after blunt in front of the apartments, while waiting for the Uber to arrive.

Ah'Million

Chapter 6
Kad

Kad stood to his feet to introduce himself to the wealthy Caucasian man sitting across from him. Little did he know, Kad knew more about him than what he was portraying. For months, he'd been doing his research on Mr. Dunbar. He had knowledge of his recent investments and his potential one.

"So, Mr." he paused. He held his old, shaky hand out.

"McVale," Kad responded quickly, as he firmly gripped his hand.

Mr. Dunbar sat back down, carefully crossing his legs.

"So, tell me exactly why I should invest in your organization."

Kad cleared his throat. "Well, Mr. Dunbar, here at Weallin, we provide children with incarcerated parents the essentials needed for everyday life, including after school programs, school supplies, as well as appearance enhancements. Lastly, we provide transportation for visitation and a therapist for any family with broken relationships, to help mend them."

Mr. Dunbar peered at Kad in silence. Inwardly, he was impressed. However, he needed to see more.

Kad was unfazed by his stoic expression. He figured he was simply assimilating the information. Before he fixed his mouth to ask, Kad retrieved the documents from the table behind him. The documents provided any numerical information he would need to back everything he just explained.

Mr. Dunbar sifted slowly through the paperwork, as if he was reading word for word and calculating every number. Suddenly, he placed the folder back on the table in front of him. He slowly stood to his feet.

"Mr. McVale, there is no need to go any further. I love what you're doing here, at Weallin, and I'm honored to assist you and your organization so you can continue the good work."

The female who had come with him handed Kad a check. Kad assumed she was his secretary. He didn't want to seem eager so he slid the check down his front pocket.

"Thank you, sir. I'm going to gladly add your name to the list of investors who helped me build and uphold the Foundation," Kad grinned.

Mr. Dunbar returned the gesture. He looked like he suffered from Parkinson's.

As the two of them disappeared around the corner, Kad became antsy. His hands trembled in anticipation. He retrieved the check from his pocket.

"Whoo!" He fist-pumped the air repeatedly. The hundred-thousand-dollar check sent a rush of excitement through him.

"What's going on Mr. McVale?" Susie, his secretary, asked, appearing concerned.

"Another one bites the dust, baby!"

He rushed towards her, lifting her off her feet. She smiled awkwardly. Kad, realizing he'd gotten carried away, placed her feet back on solid ground. Their eyes locked, longer than he intended.

Her crimson red lipstick stained her perfectly shaped lips. Images of her red lips wrapped around his pole flooded his mental. He forced his eyes shut in an attempt to rid the images, while her nipples hardened against his shoulder. He could feel her warm breath on his cheek. Her breath smelled like coffee and butterscotch. The coffee was subtle, luckily. If it hadn't been, it would've surely turned him off. One thing he despised was bad breath.

Realizing she was still in his arms, he let go hastily, and backed away. He cleared his throat.

"My bad, I got carried away," he admitted, buttoning up his blazer.

"It's fine, you have a reason to celebrate. If you need anything, I'll be at my desk."

Susie had been his secretary for nearly a month and a half, which was surprising, being that she was secretary number five. After starting the organization in 2014, Kad went three years without employees. He wasn't earning what he thought he'd earn.

So the money that he was making, he wanted it all to himself, excluding Bobby's share.

In 2017, Kad hired Tisha. She lasted two and a half years before she was fired. The casual sex started within the first year of her employment. Kad thought he could juggle both the business and personal relationship they shared. He was wrong.

After trying to figure out different ways to approach and tackle the situation, without leaving her jobless, he was exhausted. He knew what had to be done. However, he didn't want to be the bearer of the bad news, so he swayed Bobby to do it. Tisha was quiet the first few weeks. After seeing her replacement, she threw a fit, almost to the point Kad considered taking her life. The threats and harassment had simply become too much for him to endure.

One day, it all stopped. Since Tisha, there were three more. Kad tried his hardest to keep it professional, but something always happened that led to sex. Oddly, Kad never made the first move. He figured they did it to solidify their position, or simply because they wanted some dick. Little did they know, the biggest mistake was crossing the line. Instead of playing shit out and allowing things to get worse, he made sure to fire them as soon as the lines were crossed.

Susie, on the other hand, was ten years his senior and happily married, or so she portrayed.

"For you, Mr. McVale." She handed him the short glass. In one gulp, he downed the strong liquor that burned the center of his chest. His eyes met Susie's intense glare.

"Thanks." He placed the glass on the table and walked away. He just hoped she'd last longer than the average.

Ah'Million

Chapter 7
Jewel

"Baby girl, I'm sorry." Kad paused. "I had some serious business to tend to."

He rushed inside with Bobby on his heels. His pace was slower, as he strolled carelessly into her home. He was paid, sexy, and mysterious. Possessing this air of authority that sent quivers along her spine. His piercing, light brown eyes locked on hers, only for a second.

"Right, Bobby?" Kad peered over his shoulder at Bobby.

"For show," Bobby added, looking down at the screen on his phone.

"Look, baby girl, I'm going to be in my studio. I need you to do two things for me."

"What's that?" she questioned, looking pissy.

Kad smacked his lips. "Baby girl, let me make it." He paused. "Please?"

Kad wrapped his arms around his daughter, squeezing her tight. Within seconds, she burst out into laughter. It was a move Kad had done on his daughter multiple times to cheer her up.

"Okay! Okay, Dad." She giggled uncontrollably, once Kad released his arms.

"Like I was saying, an artist is coming. Show him the way to the studio." He paused.

Jewel peered past him and into the eyes of Bobby, who appeared angry.

"Secondly, use my card to order from *Wing Stop* with Door Dash. Get a variety of flavored wings, and enough fries."

Bobby disappeared down the hallway and around the corner. Jewel discreetly watched him, curious to discover the reason for his sudden vexation.

Kad looked down at his watch, then handed Jewel his bank card.

"Niece, you alright?"

"I'm good, Unc."

"Just checking. If y'all need me I'm in the studio."

Jewel did as she was told. She ordered a little more than Wing Stop. The cute boutique's outfits caught her eye. She ordered a few for herself, and a few for her favorite cousin. Myesha didn't have money to blow, nor a parent to spoil her, like Kad did Jewel. So anytime Jewel shopped, she never forgot about her cousin. A knock at the door startled the both of them.

"Who you think it is?" Myesha jolted forward.

Jewel rolled her eyes, obviously untroubled. "I've seen every one of them, so they all old news to me," she replied before heading towards the door.

She swung the door open without carefully examining her guest. However, the glimpse of him she caught, unintentionally, forced her to close the door before he could step inside.

"What is he doing here? He's the last person I expected." Her eyes widened in panic.

"I know you may not want to, but you have to let him in, Jewel. He's your dad's guest."

Jewel deeply sighed. Surrendering to the facts, she stepped to the side to allow him in. Jewel opened the door, then lowered her head.

Blotchy peered at her in confusion. "Is there a reason you closed… Hey, don't I know you?" He squinted his eyes in hopes to remember exactly where he knew her from.

"No, I don't believe so. Just come on in."

Blotchy was a bit reluctant, but he waved it off and did as he was told. Immediately, he locked eyes with Myesha. Suddenly, he remembered.

"Oh shit! Look, I was going through something." With his palms, he patted his chest. "That's my fault. Forgive me for that, shawty." He swiftly searched Jewel's face, hoping she'd look into his eyes and feel his sincerity. But her head remained low.

"It's cool, come on. They're in here."

Blotchy sighed deeply. He peered over his shoulders at Myesha. A look of defeat adorned his face, as he continued to follow

Jewel down the hallway. He thought about grabbing her arm to cease her step but reconsidered.

He stared at her big, juicy ass, while following her to the studio. She didn't appear as if she was purposely trying to hypnotize him. But the way her hips switched and her ass jiggled made Blotchy want to take her down right there in the hallway. Her upper half was petite and feminine. The back of her neck was even appealing. Her lower half was stunning. Forcing him to wonder how God created a specimen so perfect.

She stopped in front of the door, then twisted the knob, and pushed it open.

"Here you go." Her voice was low, close to a whisper. She lowered her head.

"Thank you." He peered into her eyes, hoping she would look up for a moment.

Blotchy wished to have said more. He was even hoping she'd notice the spark in his eyes. However, once he spotted Kad, and Kad spotted him, he knew all the extra would have to cease.

Jewel quickly returned to the living room with Myesha.

"I still can't believe he's inside of my house!" Jewel rushed towards Myesha and sat down next to her on the couch.

"That was awkward. His ol' rude ass." Myesha frowned, appearing irritated. "Now he want to make excuses and shit. Fuck him."

Jewel remained silent as she listened to her cousin ramble on. Just an hour ago she swore to never look his way, but all that changed in the blink of an eye. *Am I really considering him?* She wondered. Blotchy may have been downright rude to her, but a part of her was ready and willing to overlook it.

The rest of that day, Jewel was oddly quiet. His apologetic eyes were more so an image in her mind's gallery that reappeared every time she hit delete.

Myesha rambled on about Big Dooski until their lids grew heavy.

Ah'Million

Chapter 8
Bobby

"Alright, alright. We'll run it back tomorrow," Kad said to Blotchy.

He wasn't officially with the label, but it was in the making. The three of them had been in the studio since five that evening. It was now a few minutes after twelve.

"Cool, same time?" Blotchy asked. His eyes widened with eagerness. There was no denying his raw talent, but there were personal issues Blotchy possessed that Bobby simply didn't agree with.

"Same time."

He shook hands with Kad, then stuck his hand out to do the same with Bobby. However, Bobby met his open hand with a closed fist.

"Covid," he uttered, seeing the look of disdain on Blotchy's face.

Kad led Blotchy out of the house.

Bobby waited for him to return.

Kad entered, smoothly rubbing his hands together. The grin plastered across his face only irritated Bobby more.

"What's the problem, B? That young nigga hot right now. Did you hear those bars?"

"Yeah, I heard him." Bobby paused, then stood to his feet. "I'm not taking nothing from him. I just think he's more of a liability than a benefit."

Kad peered at Bobby in silence. It was proven that Blotchy was a hot head, but his love of money forced him to overlook his flaws.

"Look, I'm not trying to make it hard on you. Do what you think is best. I'm about to head out. I'll see you tomorrow." Bobby gathered his things.

"Cool, be careful, boy."

Bobby figured Kad wouldn't walk him to the door once he reclined in the leather chair and put the cup up to his lips. Since

Danielle's death, Kad had been sipping lean like it was water. Bobby made his way out of the studio and down the long, dark hallway. He scrolled down his contacts. He was looking for something wet and tight to slide in.

"Shit!" He yelled.

His and Jewel's bodies collided, forcing his phone out of his hand onto the floor. The feel of her small hand mistakenly swiping his dick made Jewel completely alert.

"I'm sorry," she apologized, bending over to retrieve his phone.

The small booty shorts exposed her perfectly round cheeks. Bobby's brows dipped in shock. He quickly turned his head to avoid gazing at her goodies.

"Here you go." She spun around. Their eyes locked.

"Thanks," Bobby grabbed his phone and proceeded past Jewel.

The awkward encounter had all sorts of things flooding his mental. His main concern was the way his body responded to the young thang. The twitch of his dick was what forced him to look away. How could he ever enjoy something so inappropriate from his best friend's seventeen-year-old daughter? The question rang out ceaselessly in Bobby's mind.

***

"Ooohh! Fuck. Nigga, I love this dick," Kesha screamed.

Her juices flowed down her thick, long legs, as Bobby pounded her from behind. He used his large hand to grip and spread her soft round ass, while enjoying the view of his manhood appear and disappear out of her small tunnel. He sexed Kesha whenever he was in heat. She was the best piece of pussy he'd come across in years, although he hated the topics she'd bring up once they were done. She matched his strokes effortlessly, as the collision of their body parts made its own tune.

Whack!

Kesha slowed down from the stinging smack, but she didn't stop. She cried out in pleasure, then bit her bottom lip. Her narrow breasts swung back and forth as Bobby plunged himself in and out of her opening. They weren't long and floppy, but after giving birth to her son years ago, they weren't as perky as they use to be.

"I'm cummin', zaddy."

Bobby loved Kesha's seductive and sensual voice. Her moans were even appealing.

"Cum on this dick then." Bobby knew he was on the verge, too. His left leg would shake ceaselessly, warning him of what was soon to come.

Kesha knew that, too. "Cum with me. You know you about to," she said breathlessly, without slowing her stride.

"Um," he moaned.

He wanted to speak, but he couldn't as he focused on pushing through his body stiffening. Veins protruded from his neck as he thrust forward, everything stiffened at once. He gave her one final thrust before the warm liquid burst out like a busted pipe.

The feeling of his seeds flowing inside of her felt good to Kesha. She wished for many nights, similar to this one, that she wasn't on birth control and she could bless Bobby with his first child.

He pulled out and lay on top of the sheets. His large dick clung to his left leg. If you didn't know any better, you would've thought he was some sort of monster that God created with three legs.

Kesha's mouth watered at the sight of it. The head was perfectly shaped, resembling a mushroom. It was a shade or two lighter than the shaft. She found it unique. She lay next to him, laying her head on his chest, while massaging his pole.

"Bobby?" She whispered, peering down at his defined abs.

"Yeah." Bobby rolled his eyes as he glared at the ceiling. He knew exactly what was on her mind. It never failed. She did it every time.

"Am I not enough for you?"

"Come on, Kesha, let's not do this."

"No, I want to do it. You avoid this shit every time. Not tonight," she cursed, sitting up straight in the bed. She peered at him intensely with her arms folded across her chest.

"Okay, talk." He jolted forward, then propped himself up against the headboard.

"Um, well, you know I been wanting to take things to the next level," she spoke timidly. Nervousness pricked through her.

"Understood." He paused. "I don't," he shrugged, without budging or breaking eye contact. His tone brooked no argument.

"Listen, I'm willing to conform to some things. I wouldn't usually conform-"

His hard gaze stopped her flow of words.

"I know that, but I'm fine with this," he simply responded, before rolling out of bed.

"So that's it?" She slid off her side of the bed and made her way around it towards him.

"For now. I'll call you." He kept getting dressed.

Kesha peered at him in disbelief through narrow slits. Bobby grabbed his keys off the nightstand and headed for the door.

"Really? Are you serious right now, Bobby?" She followed him through the house.

Luckily, her son, Prince, was at his grandmother's house as Kesha ranted and raved at Bobby in her birthday suit. Bobby stopped dead in his tracks. He spun around. They were face to face. She glared at him through flared nostrils as her chest heaved.

"You 'pose to be my peace, not disturb it."

She stared at him, a little taken aback. He tore his eyes from her tearful gaze and let himself out into the dark, wintry night.

Chapter 9
Kad

Kad activated the alarm on his 2020 SRT Charger, while heading inside the building. There was a new list of potential investors, and it was dire that he contact them personally and set up a meeting right away.

"Hey, Kad," Sierra greeted. She appeared out of nowhere, blocking the entrance.

Taken aback, he stopped dead in his tracks, giving her a quick once over. After firing Tisha, he made a commitment to himself that he'd keep his business and personal lives separate. But as soon as the hottie applied in person at his establishment, she was hired on the spot. Although she was a sight for sore eyes, he forced himself to believe that there was no physical attraction. Until one day, he walked into his office with a fully exposed Sierra sitting on top of his desk. The silk green robe was wide open, hanging off her shoulders. Her legs were spread open, giving him a clear shot of her shaven, plump, pretty pink pussy. His mug was placed right beside her.

"Here's your coffee and breakfast," she offered, patting her box. Since that day, their sex sessions continued. Of course, until she got in her feelings.

"What's up?" he greeted shortly.

"I want to talk." She inched closer.

"Of course, you're here. What do you want to talk about?"

She pursed her lips. "Why are you always so direct?"

"It keeps shit simple."

She nodded. Fidgeting with the tie on the bottom of her jacket, she struggled to speak her peace.

"Can we discuss this in your office?" Her words were laced with eagerness.

"What's wr-"

"Please?" She begged. Her eyes filled with desperation.

The ability he possessed to make someone so beautiful and strong turn to an individual so needy and weak made his dick twitch. Gazing down at the way the fitted shirt and pencil skirt hugged her curves, there was no way he could deny her request.

"Five minutes, Sierra," he lied. He knew she'd be there longer than five minutes, once the sex session began.

Her caramel complexion and deep dimples made her resemble the actress Lauren London. He marched inside with Sierra on his heels. Although she had become a serious problem since and during their split, the power of that "*P*" still allowed some consideration for her.

Susie was sitting behind her desk when Kad and the young hottie entered.

"Susie, take your lunch break," he said, without slowing his stride.

She gathered her things quickly. "Yes, sir."

Sierra shot her a dirty look, which forced her to slow her flow.

Susie sneered in confusion as she watched the young, black chick strut towards Kad's office. He placed the briefcase on top of his desk before flopping onto the leather swivel chair. His fingers were intertwined on top of his desk as he gazed at Sierra intensely.

"How could all of that ugly come from someone so beautiful?"

Her emotions had spiraled out of control, forcing her over the edge. If only she didn't allow her feelings to run away from her, things between them would still be the same. Just the thought of it made his dick harden. Sex with the young beauty was amazing. Unfortunately, nothing lasts forever.

"I would like my job back, Kad. I understand things went left." She paused. "It won't happen again. I promise."

As contrite as it seemed, He gladly refused. "Nah, Sierra, we can work on being okay outside of here. As for employment? Nah, that'll never happen."

Kad stood to his feet. He began to remove things from his briefcase. He simply felt no pity for the woman that stood before him. Her actions almost cost him greatly. He had put blood, sweat, and tears into attaining every last one of his possessions. To lose it all on account of someone else, simply wasn't an option.

"Kad, I'm sorry." She bit her lip. "For what I did."

Reluctantly, he peered into her eyes. He truly didn't give a damn if she was sorry or not.

"Do you forgive me?" she asked, walking towards him.

She wrapped her arms around his waist. Her sweet feminine scent filled his nostrils. Surrendering to her touch, he wrapped his arms around her, too. She lifted her head and gazed up at him. He pulled her tighter, his rock-hard dick jabbing her midsection.

"That's still my pussy?" he whispered, as his lips brushed her temple.

Wishing to be closer, she stood on the tips of her toes. His tongue swept into her mouth and she murmured softly. She took his mouth with passion, smothering him. Then the kiss softened, becoming almost tender. Cupping her breast, he pinched her nipple. It swelled instantly

She drew in a breath at the feel of his stiffness, then stared down at the bulge in his pants. Old memories surfaced, forcing her to lick her lips. She pulled down his zipper and slid her hands inside of his pants. As soon as her fingers wrapped around his thick pole, she tugged on it until it was fully exposed, admiring the length. You would've thought it was some sort of award the way she gawked at it in admiration.

She dropped to her knees, leaned forward, and pressed her lips to his tip. Immediately, Kad reach out and glided his fingers through her hair.

"Open your mouth," he said, his voice tight.

She opened and he drew her head down. Once the head was in, she twirled her tongue over it, then sucked. He pushed her head further down his shaft, and further. She relaxed and opened wide, allowing him to glide down her throat. He pressed forward and back, setting a rhythm. A few slow strokes, then several fast, then he slowed it down again.

His thickness stretched her little mouth. She squeezed her eyes shut to endure the aching. Feeling the corners of her mouth splitting, she slowed up a bit.

"Keep going." He gripped her hair tighter. "Come on."

She continued. Her other hand slid to his balls. She caressed them.

"Fuck!" He jerked uncontrollably as he filled her mouth with hot salty liquid.

She kept sucking as he groaned in pleasure. He fell backwards onto the leather chair. Latching on like a pit, she sucked a little longer, then drew back. She licked his limp penis, lapping at it until every drip was gone. There was even traces of cum along his testicles that she licked up, too. Once she was done, she peered up at him. Her eyes burning with desire.

He stood up, pulling her up to her feet, too. He slid everything off the top of his desk, which was a little to nothing. Gripping her by her ass, he lifted her up and placed her on top of his desk. Using his hips, he forced his way through her thick thighs and into her personal space. His eyes fell on her lace panties that did nothing to hide her flesh. He unfastened a button on her shirt, and another. Then he pulled it open, revealing her breasts. They were perky and free of blemishes. Her pecan colored areolas complimented her caramel complexion.

"Oh, so you were prepared, huh?" Kad asked, seeing that she was braless.

She moaned in agreement, as he ran his hands over her breasts, squeezing her nipples between his fingers.

"Please, fuck me," she cried.

His penis was so close to her opening that the heat from her box grazed his dick. Hearing her beg brought a smile to his face.

"Open up."

She did, and he glided his dick up and down her center.

"I'm about to fuck the shit out of you," he murmured fiercely against her ear.

He nipped her ear lobe, then thrust forward. He drove into her, stretching her pussy. She leaned back and wrapped her legs around his waist. He shifted inside her, making her moan.

"Oooh, Kad, I love this shit."

"Damn." He pulled out, then thrust forward again.

She shivered as he surged all ten inches into her again and again, stroking her tunnel.

Sierra's voice grew higher and higher, until it was a high squeal of delight.

"Whose pussy is this?" He needed to hear her say his name as bad as he needed to take his next breath.

"Kad, oooh, Kad. Please don't stop. This is your pussy."

"Come for me then," he uttered between thrust.

"Yes, I, oooh," she moaned as pleasure swept through her. "I'm coming." Her last words were almost indistinguishable between the shuddering, wheezing and cries.

His body throbbed against her, and his dick swelled, flooding her insides with hot liquid. He buried his face in her hair as his body shuddered in ecstasy. He slid out of her warmth, and she peered up at him, smiling. Satisfaction danced in her eyes. He knew she anticipated a mutual reaction, but instead, his face was drawn tight in sternness.

"I'll catch up with you later, but for now, you have to go."

Coupled with embarrassment was rejection in her piercing brown eyes. She snatched up her clothing with aggression and got dressed.

Kad placed his dick back inside his briefs and zipped up his pants.

Sierra stormed out of his office, without uttering a word. He followed her at his own pace. He approached the front desk with his hands buried in his pockets. Surprisingly, he found Susie sifting through papers. He peered down at his Vacheron Constantin, courtesy of Bobby for his thirtieth birthday.

"When did you get back?" He sneered in confusion.

She peered up at him with her left brow raised. "I never left."

His body stiffened as he gritted his teeth. He had carefully timed himself to assure this wouldn't happen. Regret pervaded through him as he lowered his head shamefully and turned to walk away.

"Mr. McVale."

He stopped dead in his tracks, then turned around and met her ocean blue eyes. "Don't be upset. You're not my preference."

"A black cup of coffee isn't shit without creamer. That's why I stick with my kind."

His left brow raised up. He was completed stunned.

She dropped her gaze onto the paperwork in front of her and continued to sift through it. Her remark shattered his ego. It was only so much he could say. Actions spoke volumes, but in this case, he would simply have to remain silent and tuck his tail. There was no way he was going to fall victim again.

Chapter 10
Myesha

Shawty go jogging every morning (every morning)/And she make me breakfast almost every morning (Every morning)/And she take a naked pic' before she leave the door/I be waking up to pics before a nigga yawning/And every weekend my shawty coming over (over)/Shawty could Fendi out, but she like Fashion Nova (Nova)/She ain't driving no Camry, she pullin' in a Rover (Rover)/With her hair so curly, I love you, baby/She said what you know 'bout love?(I'll tell you everything)/I got what you want (go get it)/You get what you please.

Myesha snapped her fingers and gyrated to the beat, as she sang along to the Pop Smoke lyrics. Big Dooski was leaned back in his seat, casually glancing in her direction, while waiting in the drive thru line for their food.

"This my shit," she yelled. She and Big Dooski had been seeing a lot of each other lately.

"Here you go." He passed her the food and drinks.

"Thank you."

"Oh, you good. Am I going to see you tomorrow?" He glanced in her direction.

"Well, I don't know. I'm supposed to be chilling with my cousin tomorrow."

"Oh, that's cool. We can all chill. You know, Blotchy want to hook up with her anyways."

Myesha didn't want to tell Dooski, but she was sure that Jewel did not want to hook up with Blotchy.

He continued to talk but the only thing she could hear was her stomach growling. She wanted badly to eat her food, but she didn't want Dooski to think anything less of her. Besides, if she entered her home with the McDonalds bag, her mother would definitely have something to say.

"Hit me up after you get settled in," he spoke smoothly. His words were laced with attitude.

Whenever she was around him, she felt secure. "Okay."

He leaned in for a kiss. He kissed her forehead, then her chin, before his mouth covered hers. His tongue tangled with hers. She wrapped her arms around him. He deepened the kiss, sending her heart soaring. He leaned back. She found herself gazing into his pecan colored eyes. She eased back. Feeling extremely self-conscious, she opened the door and slid out.

"Black, you good?" He hollered from his car as he watched her climb the steps.

She gave him a thumbs up and continued up the stairs. She peered back to see if Big Dooski had driven off. He had. She rolled the brown paper sack up tightly and shoved it down into her purse. There was no way her mother could see that.

Myesha took a deep breath before unlocking the door and letting herself in. It was pitch black inside the tiny apartment. The oven light wasn't even on. A television could be heard from a distance. It was coming from her mother's room. She didn't need light to see, being that there was only two T.V.s in the house, the one in the living room and her mother's. She eased the door closed.

"So, he gives you a wet ass and all you come back with is a happy meal?"

Myesha peered into the darkness. *How in the hell does she know about the food?*

"Mom, we didn't have sex."

"Whatever, bitch! You trash just like your trifling sisters."

Bey switched the lamp on. She sat calmly on the love seat. Her piercing stare and harsh words brought tears to Myesha's eyes. Her mother was irate, and whenever she was like this, there wasn't any limits to what she might do or say.

"I'm not lying to you, momma. He's just my friend." Tears rolled down her cheeks. Myesha gritted her teeth to cease the chattering. Her mother stood to her feet.

"Get naked," she demanded.

"Wh-why, momma?" Fear filled her, forcing her to stammer.

"Don't question me in my shit. Get naked!" she yelled.

Myesha's body shook uncontrollably as she tried discerning her mother's motive by peering into her apathetic eyes. Ceaseless sniffles filled the apartment. She removed her Ugg boots first. Kad had bought them for her last Christmas. Unbuckling her belt, then unfastening her pants, she slid the zipper down and wiggled out of the tight Levi's.

A creaking sound forced her to freeze in terror. There was company. The sound of his foot dragging across the hardwood floor helped confirm her speculation. She cringed at the sight of him, as soon as he came into view.

"What are you waiting on girl?" Bey continued, as if her fifty-year-old boyfriend wasn't standing behind her, trying to see her seventeen-year-old daughter's body parts.

"But your, your boy-boyfriend." Myesha pointed.

Bey looked over her shoulders then back at Myesha.

"That's my nigga! He's not worried about your young ass. Do as I say before I do it myself." Her eyes widened as she inched closer.

Myesha felt so violated. She gritted her teeth to contain her composure.

"Really, momma?" She questioned in disbelief.

"Really," she responded through clenched teeth.

Myesha peered at her mother's disabled boyfriend unblinkingly as she shimmied out of her jeans. The sight of her hairy pussy made him lick his lips. She pursed her lips as the tears descended freely.

Her mother kneeled before her. She used her thumbs to pry her lips apart, then moved closer to sniff her private area. Myesha kept her eyes trained on her mother's boyfriend. He smirked at her mischievously, while massaging his dick. Her ignorant mother was oblivious to it all. She stood to her feet.

"He probably didn't fuck you this time 'cause his momma was home. I wouldn't fuck you if I had a dick, smelling like that." She paused "Go get your musty pussy ass in the shower!"

Myesha gasped sharply and then bent down and pulled up her jeans. Her jaws clenching so tightly that they begin to hurt. She snatched her boots and purse from the floor and darted towards her room, brushing past her mother's sick boyfriend. She'd never felt humiliation to such degree.

Chapter 11
Jewel

"Ms. McVale?"

Jewel jolted at the sound of her name. She tore her eyes from her phone and up ahead at her English teacher, Ms. Winter.

"Ma'am?" Nearly every student in class peered in her direction.

"Come here, please."

Jewel slowly stood to her feet. She hoped whatever it was Ms. Winter wanted to discuss, it didn't extend past school hours. This was her last class of the day and she was drained, ready to go home.

"I read your essay," she paused. "It was quite interesting," she admitted, her hands clasped on top of the desk.

"Thanks," Jewel smiled. Her mother use to praise her all the time for her writing ability. Since losing her, it had been a minute since she heard anything similar.

"The counselor notified me of the arrival of your transcripts." She retrieved them from her drawer. "You're a credit shy from your Associates Degree."

Jewel covered her head as tears threaten to emerge. Her mother had sacrificed so much to put her in the private school, and even more to keep her there. Unfortunately, it wasn't enough.

"I'm aware of that," she admitted, as she peered around aimlessly.

"Unfortunately, we don't offer those courses."

Jewel sneered at her in confusion.

"However, I can give you the location to where they are offered. An oncologist is a hell of choice, don't you agree?"

Jewel shrugged. "You can say that, I guess."

"It has to be a story behind it. I find it unlikely that at the age of six you told your parents you'd like to be an oncologist when you're older," she assumed.

Danielle's death was a touchy subject for Jewel. Jewel smacked her teeth, not hiding her reluctance or irritation at all.

"Look, I'm saying all this to say, study hard so you can excel on your SAT. The opportunity like the one you have doesn't happen too often."

Jewel opened her mouth to speak, afraid she offended Ms. Winter, but the sound of the bell diverted her attention.

"Thanks, Ms. Winter. Later." She retrieved her things and zoomed out of the classroom, bumping into someone right outside the door. "Excuse me," she apologized quickly.

The girl spun around, sneering at Jewel in disgust. "Say, watch out, lil bitch," she spat.

Jewel leaned back, appalled. "Damn, I said excuse me. But it's cool, you got it," she said calmly, while backing away.

"What you say?" she questioned, removing her book bag and allowing it to fall beside her.

Jewel's lips quivered and panic seeped in. The chick moved in closer.

"I didn't say—"

Whap! Whap!

Myesha's fist flew past Jewel's head, connecting with the girl's face. She swung with speed and precision, forcing the girl to stumble backwards. She palmed her cheek, while eyeing Myesha in disbelief.

"What the fuck, Myesha?"

"What? This my motherfucking cousin! Don't talk now! Run up on me like you did her!" Myesha rocked back and forth with her arms by her side, moving in a circular motion. The girl reached down to pick up her bag.

"Girl, I'm not about to fight you. We better than that."

"Ha!" she laughed sinisterly. Myesha had been distant the past two days, but she had shown up at the perfect time.

"If we were so close, you would've known this was my cousin. Plea bargain with the judge. The only deal I got for you is this ass whoopin'."

The chick smacked her lips. "Whatever."

Before she could turn and walk away, Myesha lunged forward, striking her in the side of the face. Once she connected with the right hook, the chick threw her arms up in an attempt to block the other blows.

Bink! Bink!

A left and right uppercut sent her crashing on her back. Myesha lifted her leg and stomped the girl in the ribs repeatedly.

"Myesha! That's enough," Jewel screamed.

Myesha stopped, then peered at her cousin. The demented look in her eyes sent quivers down Jewel's spine. Coupled with fear was shock. She had never seen Myesha move so violently. Myesha kicked the girl one last time in the abdomen.

"Now I'm cool," she announced, draping one arm over Jewel's shoulder. They exited the building together.

"Want to go half on some Kush and chill at my house?

"I really have to study, Myesha."

The girls eased around and through the traffic in front of the school building.

"Study what?" Myesha stopped moving, awaiting Jewel's response.

"The S.A.T."

"S.A.T.?"

"Yeah, I was taking college courses at my other school. I'm a credit away from finishing."

"Girl, please." Myesha waved her hand dismissively. "Bitches out the hood don't make it to college. Come on." She dragged Jewel across the street towards the parking lot.

Jewel would usually contemplate on Myesha's negative statements, but this one wasn't going to even get a second thought. College was her mother's only wish, and she was determined to fulfill just that.

Ah'Million

Chapter 12
Blotchy

Big Dooski sat in the passenger seat, smoking on the loud that filled Blotchy's black on black G wagon. They had been in the lot for almost ten minutes now. He lifted the cup full of codeine to his lips as he waited for the pretty young thang to emerge. Jewel had been on his mind since the night she led him to the studio inside of her house. Her beauty was breathtaking.

Although he was furious the day they exchanged words inside his store, he couldn't deny her beauty then. She had some of the most angelic and feminine features he'd ever seen. Her hazel eyes, caramel skin, and juicy booty were simply images he couldn't delete out of his memory bank.

"Ha! This lil bitch got you stalking her." Big Dooski puffed on the blunt.

"Stalking?" Blotchy paused. "I don't even know what that shit is."

"Nah, on some real shit. Remember ol' boy you beefed with inside the sto'?"

"Yeah, what about him?" Blotchy inquired, peering into Big Dooski's eyes.

"He talking. Say he gon' catch us in the sto' and air the whole bitch out."

Blotchy burst into laughter.

Big Dooski pulled hard on the blunt. This time the smoke curled up. Blotchy's unconcerned response vexed him deeply. Underestimating the opp was how niggas got popped.

The students filed out of the school building, groups at a time. He stretched his neck to help him see, but it was no use.

"I'll be back," Blotchy announced, hopping out of the truck.

His eyes moved swiftly, and his legs barely moved at all. There she was. His lips turned up in a smile. He stepped to the side, placing himself directly in her path.

"What's up?"

"Hey," she responded, giving Blotchy a quick once over.

"Look, I-"

"Hey, Blotchy! Ooohh. Bitch, that's Blotchy!" The trio of young girls waved in unison.

Politely, he waved back.

"Come on, Myesha, I don't have time for this." Jewel grabbed Myesha's forearm and jerked her forward.

Blotchy stood in their way. There was no way he was letting Jewel get away from him.

"What's the rush?"

"That's my business," Jewel shot back.

"Myesha," Big Dooski yelled, walking around the truck

"Dooski!" She ran and wrapped her arms around him, like she hadn't seen him in forever.

"Come on, don't be rude."

"Rude? The way you talked to me at your store, and I'm rude?" In spite of the aggression, her voice was soft, posing no threat. Her button nose flared. She was upset, yet undeniably gorgeous.

"You right. I apologize."

"Tuh," Jewel rolled her eyes. Anyone with ears could tell he was bullshitting.

"I know you don't trust me because you don't know me. Sincerity is my only credential."

Their eyes locked. Her once stiff shoulders slumped. She peered at Myesha, then back at Blotchy.

"Aye, lil' momma. Please forgive him. I'm hungry," Big Dooski hollered from a few feet away.

Blotchy clasped his hands together, as if he was praying. Reluctantly, she smiled.

"Yeah, okay."

***

"So, this is where you spend most of your time?" Jewel asked, sitting beside him, Indian style, on the sofa.

He glared at her unblinkingly. Admiration danced behind his irises as their conversation flowed effortlessly.

"Pretty much, if I'm not at the smoke shop." He shrugged.

After grabbing a bite to eat, the four of them got comfortable inside the spacious suite, which Blotchy referred to as his 'studio.' He could tell by the darkening of Jewel's lips that she smoked weed. A few blunts of Kush in rotation, and she slowly loosened up. She chuckled, peering around in satisfaction.

"I can tell." She paused. "It's real homely."

"Homely?" What you mean by that?"

"It's," she smacked her lips. "I don't know exactly how to word it, but it's different than most studios I've seen. The sofa, mini fridge, shower," she paused, pursing her lips. "Air mattress." She smiled. "It just has a cozy setting. That's it, that's all."

Blotchy appeared to be attentive. However, he hadn't heard a word she said. His gazed was fixed on her pretty plump lips. He was imagining them around his dick.

"Hello," Jewel said, waving her hand from side to side, trying to get his attention.

"My bad. That weed and drank ain't no joke." He chuckled nervously.

"So, do you have any siblings?" She asked. She cut her eyes in the direction where Myesha and Dooski were sneaking off to.

Blotchy followed her eyes. Envy filled him, seeing his friend creep off into a more secluded place.

"Are you and Big Dooski related?"

"Nah, Big Dooski is just my homie. We been cool since elementary. I love him like a brother, and I trust him with my life." He cleared his throat. "I do, well I did have a younger brother. He-" The ringing of Jewel's phone ceased his speech.

Her eyes widened as she peered down at her screen. "Shit, it's my dad," she cursed. Her eyes roamed frantically.

"What's up? When is your curfew?" he asked curiously. "It's not even six." He peered down at his iPhone.

"My dad is just strict. He likes to know my every move." She held up a finger to silence him.

"Hey, dad," she answered, sounding unfazed, although her nerves were shot. She peered up at Blotchy, terror danced in her eyes.

"Oh, I'm at the mall. Re-remember, I asked yesterday."

Blotchy chewed his nails wishing he could hear what her father was saying. Her facial expressions would have to suffice.

"Okay," she paused. "Okay, dad." Slowly she lowered the phone from her ear.

"What's up?" Blotchy questioned, as soon as she ended the call.

"I have to go." Disappointment etched across her face.

Blotchy fumed. He was more upset than she was. "Damn, he really tripping? Bruh, you seventeen!"

"Calm down. That's my father," she shot back.

Realizing he was being a bit irrational, he leaned back on the sofa. He was horny and irritated, ready to test the treasure that hid between her slit.

She stood to her feet. "I'm going to call an Uber. Knowing my dad, he'll probably be waiting in the front yard."

He sneered offensively. There was no way he was going to give another nigga the opportunity to catch and bag his chick. Jewel was rare and fresh. Her innocence was evident. There was no way she would remain taintless. The pretty ones were always the first ones to end up corrupt. Blotchy was aroused at the idea of him being the first one to do so.

Chapter 13
Kad

Since the day Sierra flew out of Kad's office, things between him and Susie had been quite awkward. Even though neither of them touched the sensitive subject, Susie pranced around with a boost of confidence she hadn't displayed since that day. But Kad didn't think too much of it. However, a part of him was skeptical about how it stemmed. He was unsure how Susie felt about picking back up on the conversation, but he surely wanted to. Oddly, he wanted to know more about her sex life and convince her otherwise, even if it meant him showing rather than telling.

Sexually, Kad always felt like he was God's gift to women. But since the altercation between him and Susie, he had been second guessing his ability.

"Here's your coffee sir. I'll be at my desk."

Kad gazed at her lips, unable to tear his eyes away from them. A crimson red coated them, making them appear succulent and poutier. He bit down on his lips to keep from impulsively speaking his mind. A burning desire filled him. He wanted to stretch that small mouth of hers. Any other time, her silence was requested. Lately, it had become annoying. A whisper, a sound, anything other than work related things to address the elephant in the room. When it came to women, Kad never had a problem getting what he wanted. Women threw themselves at him. Susie, on the other hand, operated different.

"Shit," she cursed in a low tone, close to a whisper. It was so low that if Kad wasn't praying silently to hear her utter a word, he wouldn't've heard it. With her back to him, her head moved swiftly as she scanned the floor for something.

"Did you lose something?" He stood to his feet.

"I lost my earring," she replied. Fear laced her words. She bent over at the waist to get a closer look.

Standing as still as a statue, he admired her shapely ass from behind, his dick hardening by the second.

"I felt it fall, it has to be somewhere right here."

Don't do it, Kad. Don't do it Kad.

Knowing the bullshit that came along with fucking his secretary, Kad simply couldn't control himself. He strolled closer. Nervousness prickled through him the closer he got. The fear of rejection surfaced, forcing him to swallow the lump in his throat.

"You looking for this?" Kad pressed his hard erection against her ass. The obsession with proving her wrong taunted him like no other. Her outlook on sex with black men was completely wrong, and he planned to be the first one to show her.

She slowly lifted up and turned around. "Don't you think you're being a little unprofessional? She asked. However, her eyes said the total opposite of her unconvincing concern.

She smiled, revealing her pearly whites. Her eyes full of desire as she traced those lips with her thick tongue. He pulled her into his chest. Passion flared between them.

"Fuck what you talking about. You're about to give me some of this pussy." He leaned in and kissed her soft lips with a wet, slow peck. "Put ya hands on the desk?"

Without hesitation, she leaned onto the desk. Kad used his leg to spread her legs further apart. He aggressively lifted her skirt, just a tad bit above her ass. He yanked his Armani pants and Ethika briefs down in one swift motion, exposing his thick and caramel wrapped ten-inch pole. Cupping both her ass cheeks, he massaged them roughly. He released his grip and guided his pole up and down the crack of her ass.

The pressure of his tip against her slickness altered her breathing. He dipped, perfectly positioning himself, as he inserted himself inside of her. She opened slipping around him, inviting him inside. She moaned loudly as she fell into the piercing pleasure of Kad's lengthy pole, drilling slowly deep inside her warmth. He spread both her ass cheeks as he hammered away.

"This the best dick you ever had, huh?"

It was so pleasurable she couldn't open her mouth to respond. He spun her around and lifted her off of her feet and onto his pole.

"Ssss" she hissed. She tightened her muscles around his steel, as he dug deeper.

His dick, stretching her wide, sent a thrill through her. He grunted, while pushing deeper, stroking her craving passage with every inch.

"You like this dick, huh?"

"No, I love it. I love the way you feel inside of me."

He held her tight to him. Their bodies joined as they both wheezed. He covered her mouth with his, thrusting his tongue into her mouth. She sucked it, trying to pull it deeper. He lifted her by the ass, easing her off his dick. As soon as she thought it was over, he yanked her down onto his pole… again.

"Oh, yes."

Her head fell back in ecstasy. Pleasure pervaded through her as he did it again, then again. She quivered at the feel of his rock-hard penis cramming her small box. His strokes deepened and she moaned at the building bliss. An orgasm was merely a stroke away.

"Cum for me," he murmured against her ear, his soft, warm breath almost enough to drive her over the edge.

"Yes, make me cum then."

"Not yet." He slowed his strokes.

She released a soft, but sexy, whimper.

"Don't cum until I tell you."

Using the wall as leverage, he placed her back against it, parting her cheeks. Then he picked up his pace. With his large hands, he took control of his own thrusts.

She could tell he was on the brink of cumming by the way his dick pulsated inside of her. She clung to him, her eye lids closing as she lost herself in the overflowing satisfaction.

"Don't close your eyes. I want to see them when you cum."

Her eyelids fluttered open and she found herself peering into his chocolate eyes. He jabbed again, and she shuddered. Pleasure burst inside of her. His next thrust released the urgency inside of her and sent her into a mind blowing orgasm.

"What's my name?"

"Kad," she said weakly as the orgasm lingered inside of her. "This the best dick I ever had."

She wrapped her arms around his neck. He groaned, then drove deeper. Grunts of pleasure escaped his lips as he pulled out, releasing his seed on her thigh.

***

"Hey, hunny!" Kad announced upon entering his home. Jewel appeared engrossed in the papers laid out before her.

"Hey, dad." She spoke without looking up. Since attending the new high school and hanging around Myesha more, Jewel had lost focus in pursuing her dream. Kad dropped his briefcase onto the couch and sat beside his daughter.

"Time has just flown by," he commented, gazing at his baby girl.

Jewel finally tore her eyes from the books and peered over her shoulder at her father. To anyone else, Kad may have appeared fine, but Jewel instantly spotted the fatigue. He worked ceaselessly to ensure that they would never have days like the unfortunate ones in the past. Which must've been traumatizing, due to the fact he was now a six-figure nigga and grinding like he had lint in his pocket.

"Dad, I don't think it's smart to stay here and attend a community college." She paused. "I want to go off to a university." She lowered her head.

"Why is that?" Kad was quite stunned, but he didn't display how he truly felt.

"I don't want to get stuck here, dad. I don't want to chance anything happening that's going to trap me here and force me to lose sight of my goal," she answered. Confidence laced her words.

Kad draped his arm over her shoulder, pulling her in to his chest. "I love you, baby girl." He was elated with her appetite for success. He released her, then asked, "You hungry? I'll make us something. Just relax."

She rushed to put up her paperwork, then dashed towards the kitchen. Kad unbuttoned his shirt.

Bzz! Bzz!

He peered down at Bobby's name on the screen of his phone.

"What's up, boy?"

"Murder's second album, *The Wait Is Over*, debuted number two on the Billboard 200."

A slow smile crept onto Kad's face. Things were going well. Murder and Lil Stacks were the only artists still signed with the label. The others fizzled out.

"Where you at?"

"I'm on my way."

"Bet."

Not every artist had the same ambition as Murder and Lil Stacks. Those types of disappointments were frustrating, especially when you feel a certain sense of responsibility for someone else's success.

Beep! Beep! Beep!

Kad peered around in bewilderment at the sound of the smoke alarm. He raced towards the kitchen.

Jewel wagged her arms wildly, in an attempt to clear the smoke. Kad chuckled lightly, watching his daughter from the threshold.

"What's funny?" she asked, agitated.

Bing!

"Nothing. Let Bobby in. I'll take over."

The mentioning of Bobby's name caused Jewels eyes to widen to twice they're size. Luckily, her back was to her father. Pretending to appear normal, she dragged out of the kitchen. Once she was out of Kad's sight, she patted her bundles in place as she walked swiftly to the front door.

"Hey, Bobby," she greeted. His devastating good looks and air of authority made her heart flutter every time she saw him.

"What's up?"

She moved to the side, allowing him access into her home.

"What y'all burning?" he asked.

"That's Jewel's ass," Kad intervened.

"Good thing I brought pizza."

"It sure is, 'cause I'm starving."

Kad took the pizzas out of Bobby's hand and headed towards the kitchen. Bobby joined Kad inside of the kitchen for pizza, where they discussed their artists and music. Jewel grabbed a few slices for herself, and trotted to her room, leaving the two men alone to discuss business.

"We straight without him." Bobby spoke in reference to Blotchy.

"He has talent and potential, Bobby."

"True, but he's also a liability. You have to evaluate a person based on their character, not just talent."

Chapter 14
Myesha

"She know she's out of line for that synthetic lace," Myesha scolded, bypassing the timid looking freshman.

"She probably don't have the money for a good one," Jewel commented, peering back at the younger chick.

There were two forms of gossiping in Jewel's eyes, talking about shit, and talking about people. Talking about people was something Jewel didn't do. She was taught at a young age to say good things or nothing at all.

"How's things with you and Big Dooski?" she asked, changing the subject.

"Girl, he is so sweet. I'm really feeling him," Myesha admitted.

"That's what's up."

Jewel thought Big Dooski was going to be someone who would mistreat Myesha, but he ended up being the total opposite. The girls continued to chat as they headed towards Myesha's place. The front door was open, like it was so many other days when Jewel and Myesha arrived. Bey and her home girl, Lisa, could be heard from a distance. Myesha scoffed at the sound of the women. Jewel, on the other hand, couldn't wait to get in.

"Hey, niece," Bey yelled, once spotting the girls.

Myesha continued to her room. She acknowledged no one, and no one acknowledged her. Upon detecting the tension, Lisa nudged Bey in her side, looking in the direction Myesha had disappeared to.

"Hey, Aunt Bey!" Jewel wrapped her arms around Bey's neck, then took a step back and peered down the hallway towards Myesha room.

"Fuck that bitch. She'll live. She better be worried about securing a bag so she can get her own shit," Bey announced, killing both Lisa and Jewel's suspicion.

"Really, momma?" Myesha rushed from the rear of the house. Really Momma, what?"

"You took my door?" she asked in shock.

"Off the motherfucking hinges. This my shit," Bey shot back daringly. Her eyes squinted and nostrils flared.

Without uttering another word, Myesha headed in the direction she had come from. Numerous times, she had complained about her mother's antics, but this time, Jewel believed, topped all the rest.

"Here, niece, sit down." Bey handed Jewel the blunt.

Jewel wasted no time getting comfortable and flopping onto the sofa. She hit the blunt twice and passed it to Lisa.

"So, what's up, niecy?" Bey asked, snooping.

"I'm chillin', aunty, just trying to stay focused." Jewel may have indulged in meaningless things here and there, but nothing compared to the dedication she had towards becoming an oncologist.

"I asked 'cause you over there glowing and shit."

Jewel chuckled. Her aunty was right. She and Blotchy had been texting back and forth since the day he invited her inside his studio.

"You like him?" she asked in between puffs.

Jewel waved her aunt off, signaling that she didn't want the doobie. The last time she smoked a doobie with Myesha, it burned the tip of her freshly manicured nails. The last thing she wanted was her father to find out she smoked weed. Seeing that the weed was almost gone, she removed the gram from her bra and began to roll it up.

"I do, aunty, I really do."

"He got money?"

"Humph," Lisa grunted.

"He sure do, a lot of it."

"Let me tell you something, niece." She paused, pulling hard on the doobie one last time before smashing it into the ashtray. She leaned in closer. "Have y'all had sex?"

Jewel hurriedly shook her head. Sex was the furthest from her mind, so she thought.

"Good. But once you do, always take care of your man before he leaves the house." She paused. "Cause it's a hoe born every day."

Lisa laughed hysterically as she rocked back and forth.

Jewel chuckled, too. She thought her aunt, Bey, was the craziest and funniest person in the world. The weed grinder rolled underneath the love seat Lisa sat on.

"Lisa, get down there and hand me that grinder."

Lisa looked around dumbfounded. "Bitch, I need my knees. I got a man at home."

"What that supposed to mean? I do too! Shit, knees or no knees, I'll handle my business on nubs if need be," Bey shot back.

Jewel burst into laughter. "I'll get it," she offered.

"Yea, but I need to be at my full potential. Can't let these young girls outdo me."

"You saw on that Olympics those lil chicks *Simone Biles* and Sun Lee, *Sou Lee*, whatever the hell her name is, jumping 19ft in the air, running around like lil ninjas. They sucking dick on a handstand now-a-days."

Jewel and Lisa burst out laughing.

Ring. Ring. Ring.

Jewel peered down at her screen. It was her father calling.

"Hey, dad," she answered abruptly.

"I'm out here, baby girl."

"Ok. I'll be out in a minute." She ended the call.

"Aunt Bey, y'all can have this, but I have to go. I'll see you tomorrow." Jewel handed them the blunt and raced to Myesha's room.

Walking in without opening the door felt a little awkward to Jewel, but she shrugged it off.

"My- What's wrong?" Jewel rushed to her side.

Myesha swiped the remainder of the tears away. She wanted severely to tell her cousin exactly what she was going through, but she didn't want to destroy the image Jewel had painted of her mother. Although Myesha envied their relationship, she wasn't a hater. Like everything else she disagreed with, she held it in.

"I'm just tired of living like this," she uttered weakly.

"I know, baby. We grown now. We don't have to deal with it anymore. Come to college with me. Get away from here. It'll be fun," Jewel spoke quickly, filled with excitement.

Myesha looked Jewel directly into her eyes. "Baby girl, those are your dreams, not mine."

Honk. Honk.

"You right, but I'll call you when I get home."

"I'll walk you to the car," Myesha said, getting out of her bed.

Jewel said her goodbyes and left, with Myesha on her heels.

"Hey, before I forget, Big Dooski and Blotchy having a party Saturday. You going?"

Jewel thought hard before answering. Lately, she had been off her game.

"Nah, I have to study." She reached for the handle to her dad's car.

"Please," Myesha begged. "We don't have to stay long," she continued.

Jewel didn't want to upset Myesha any more than she already was, so she finally agreed.

"Okay." She hopped inside her dad's truck.

"Hey, Uncle Kad." Myesha waved from the curb.

"Hey, Myesha!" Jewel and Kad drove off.

She wished she could have gone, too, but didn't want to wear out her welcome. Although, no one seemed to have a problem with it, except her mother. The windy weather forced Myesha to cross her arms at her chest as she headed back inside.

"Myesha!"

She turned around and eyed her mother's new beau curiously.

"What?" she answered rudely.

"I'm, I'm sorry. Can you help me get these bags out to take them inside?" he asked, stammering over his words. He stood next to his car timidly as Myesha approached him without speaking a word.

Myesha walked over and stood in between him and the door of his car. Then she bent down and retrieved the bags.

Um, um, um," he grunted, standing behind her.

"Pervert ass," Myesha mumbled, turning around to face him.

Indeed, he wanted her in the worst way, but he tried his hardest not to come on so strong. Myesha marched inside her house, where her mother and friend were getting lit.

"Where have y-" Bey's words were cut short at the sight of her man.

"Vincent, when did you get here?" She jumped to her feet, taking the grocery bags from his hands. She treated his broke down ass like a king.

"Lisa, times up, baby. I'll catch you tomorrow," Bey hollered from the kitchen.

"Damn, bitch, we just fired up the blunt," Lisa objected. "You can take it with you, my man here. The only pussy that's going to be sitting up under him is mine. That bitch better be lucky she stay here, or hers won't be up under him neither."

"Girl, boo, you buggin'. I got my own nigga."

"Good. Go home to him." Bey didn't play about her money, meaning she surely didn't play about her man, because he was the one with the bag.

Securing a bag was Bey's ultimate goal. She didn't care who she crossed or stepped on to assure that.

"Tuh." Lisa gathered her things, which was little to nothing. Lisa depended on a man, too. The only difference was that her man was an addict, and his drug of choice was crack. He was just a functioning addict. He hustled hard to pay the rent and supply both of their habits. Lisa had no friends because she didn't have much to offer. However, her and Bey kicked it off years ago and had been getting along just fine. Lisa knew Bey meant no harm. She was simply absurd at times. Unlike most people, she understood her.

Once Lisa approached the front door, Bey said, "Call me."

"As soon as I get settled."

Myesha got tired of peering out of her window in her bedroom, so she decided to go to the living room and watch TV. Growing up, Myesha nor her sisters had TVs in their bedroom.

Bey didn't want them getting comfortable, knowing one day they'd have to assist her with the bills, or simply get out.

Big Dooski had become the seasoning to her food, a breath of fresh air. He made her days so much brighter and she fell deeper in lust as the days passed. The opportunity for them to sexually explore each other's bodies had surfaced many times, but Myesha wanted to wait for the perfect time. Big Dooski was cool with that.

She turned on the television. The new TV series "Queen" was on. She watched it while texting back and forth with Big Dooski. She yawned then stretched out on the sofa. Somewhere down the line, she fell asleep.

Low grunts slowly forced Myesha's eyes open. At first, she thought it was just a dream, so she blinked rapidly then opened them again. Vincent stood a distance away, next to the love seat, jerking his semi-hard erection. He tugged and pulled on it with his eyes closed and head tilted back. He began jerking violently. Myesha was certain he was going to fall. Veins protruded from his forehead, neck, and arms, scaring Myesha. She forced her eyes shut, hoping he'd go away.

Seconds later, when she opened her eyes, he was gone. She gasped suddenly, then jerked forward, peering around the empty, dark living room. She knew it wasn't a dream. She was awake and he was there. She knew it.

Chapter 15
Jewel

Saturday Night

"Dad, we ready," Jewel yelled from the front door. She flew down the steps and towards Kad's car as she waited for him to emerge from the house, Louis Vuitton Duffel bag in hand, filled with some apparel her father would never approve of.

Kad locked the front door and descended the steps. He appeared to be seriously engrossed with the person on the other end of the receiver. They both climbed inside the truck. Even though her dad was acting a bit strange, she had no desire to pry into his business, when she struggled with the voices inside of her head. Jewel had never lied to her father, until today.

The ride to Myesha's was soundless. Kad was so preoccupied, mentally, that even after the call was disconnected, he never considered listening to music.

"I love you, Dad," Jewel professed before climbing out of the truck.

"Jewel." He paused, looking straight ahead. He turned to face her. "Stay out of trouble. I'll be here to pick you up tomorrow, once I leave work."

Kad's tone scared Jewel. His lingering stare made her uneasy. "Okay, Dad." She hopped out. Once his car vanished around the corner, Jewel was able to breathe again.

"Hey, Cuzzo," Myesha greeted.

Music blared from the speakers as Jewel entered their small apartment. Her brows dipped in confusion as she peered around for her Aunt Bey.

"You looking for ya' home girl?" Myesha joked.

It was either her makeup, or she was under the influence, which made her eyes look slanty.

"Yeah. Where she at?"

"She gone with her little boyfriend. Let's get dressed and leave before she gets her."

"Cool."

***

"I can't wear the shit you bitches wear,
'Cause it's cheap to me.
It's some money at my table, grab a seat with me.
Cost a ticket just to cover all my legal fees.
I don't hang with jealous bitches, that's a weak disease.
Ho, don't run.
If you broke and in my business, then just shut up (sssh)
I invested in my body. Bitch, I'm done up.
I look good, like to fuck him when the sun up (oh).
I put my jewelry just to go to the bodega.
And I keep it with me just so that I'm feeling safer.
Fendi on my body, but my feet is in Bottega.
Bitch, I'm getting money. Get the fuck up outta here."

Jewel and Myesha Diddy bopped through the party, like they owned the place. Although they both would've been draped in Fendi, courtesy of Kad, they opted for a cute boutique fit instead.

Jewel sported a bedazzled crop top and matching colored skirt with the high slit, which went perfectly with her Stuart Weitzman heels. Her natural face beat was beat to perfection, giving her a glow, as if she had been kissed by the sun. Slowly and seductively she strutted her shit. Her caramel colored eyes led the way, as she scanned the crowd for one person.

The crowd began to part like the red sea for Jewel and Myesha. Myesha wore a Denim body suit with a pair of brown thigh high boots.

"I see you poking," Jewel commented on her butt.

"You see me, girl?" she shot back, then slapped her own ass.

The canary yellow eye shadow complimented her dark skin. The shimmery highlight gave her an exotic touch. Jewel peered around at everyone else and began to feel overdressed.

"Damn, this ain't Coachella," Blotchy yelled as he approached them, confirming Jewel's suspicion.

She reached up, wrapping her arms around his neck. He squeezed her waist, then inched lower and gripped Jewel's juicy ass. His cologne invaded her nostrils, forcing her to relax.

Blotchy looked mouthwatering. His Versace jeans sagged low enough to expose the print through his navy blue briefs. His muscle shirt hugged his toned chest and displayed his big shoulders and muscular arms.

"Damn," was all Jewel could say, eyeing him as if she was the lion and he was prey.

He led Jewel deeper into the house. Oddly, a sofa sat in the middle of the kitchen. A group of men huddled up in a corner, shooting dice. Jewel had seen many dice games around the way from her school, but this one was the biggest she'd ever seen.

Blotchy was determined to get some pussy tonight. He didn't give a damn what it took. A part of him didn't give a damn who it was from, but he was hoping it'd be the hottie that sat next to him. The three of them sat on the sofa.

"Man, you been on a nigga mind so heavy. I been having to keep this loud in rotation, just so I can think straight."

Although Blotchy was gaming her up, Jewel giggled like the school girl she was.

"Myesha!"

Hearing Myesha's name being called tore Jewel's eyes away from Blotchy.

Myesha smacked her lips and rushed towards Big Dooski. "I was looking for you!" She bent over and wrapped her arms around his neck.

Big Dooski hugged her back with one arm. From where Jewel sat, she could barely see the big dude squatted down in the midst of the crowd and commotion.

"Squat next to me and rake it up while I take these nigga's money."

Just like that, Myesha was out of sight. The crowd was so massive that you would've had to be close to get a good look at everything that was taking place.

"Don't worry 'bout them, bae. Focus on us," Blotchy said, using his hand to turn Jewel's head in his direction.

The smell of weed and liquor invaded her nostrils. Masculinity, with a pinch of sweetness, briefly described the mixture, as their tongues danced.

"Sit right here on my lap, since all these ho's want to low key watch a nigga."

Jewel peered around, catching a few glances. She may have been the center of attention tonight, and perhaps previous nights, but Jewel despised being in such spotlight. Slowly, she stood to her feet, discreetly covering her exposed flesh, afraid of those watching her and the things being said. Timidly she leaned against his thigh.

"Girl, come on and get yo' thick ass up here." Blotchy yanked Jewel closer, then forced her onto his lap.

He pulled the lit blunt from the ashtray beside him and held the blunt inside his palm. He placed the lit side in his mouth and held it with his teeth. Then he tilted his head, signaling Jewel to come closer.

She wrapped her big lips round the other end. Blotchy blew the shotgun smoke into her mouth, and she sucked it like a champ. Feeling as if they were in a world of their own, Blotchy's mans began to harden, as he peered into Jewel's big, light brown eyes. She pulled back, licking her succulent lips. He handed her his drink, a short glass full of brown liquid.

"I don't drink, Blotchy," she declined.

"It's just a little Hen. Take a sip," he urged.

She tossed it back, finishing the drink in two gulps. Blotchy relieved her of the now empty glass and sat it on the table beside the sofa. He grabbed her hand and placed it on his dick. The size frightened Jewel, nearly making her snatch back. But her aunt had already given her advice on how to treat a made nigga. *As long as he got something, he's worth keeping around.*

Jewel was tired of fantasizing and masturbating. She was ready for the real thing. She was ready to become a woman. She massaged his length through his briefs. Blotchy bit down on his lip, instantly soaking her panties.

"Alright, you better not wake that beast if you can't tame him."

His stare was so impassioned that it made Jewel want to take him down right there. He snaked his hand under her skirt discreetly and slid her panties to one side. It all happened so fast Jewel couldn't even protest. He stuck two fingers into her warmth.

"Damn, I make you feel like this?" he asked, referring to the pool between her legs. His fingers were drenched, as if he stuck his hands in a jar of honey.

Jewel moaned softly and seductively as he moved inside her walls and onto her growing clit.

"Fuck this. You done turned a nigga all the way up."

He eased Jewel off his lap and leaped to his feet. By now, Jewel was buzzed and ready to see what it do. He grabbed her by the hand and led the way down the hall and upstairs to a room, off to the left. Blotchy was so eager to get the pussy, he didn't even finesse her out of her clothes.

"Strip," was all he said before he yanked his briefs and jeans down in one swift motion.

The sight of his erection made Jewel's mouth water. She quickly removed one piece at a time. Blotchy pinched the tip of his dick, then stroked it, while watching her undress. Eager to show him what she had learned on porn hub, she dropped to her knees. Stunned, he peered at her approvingly.

"Let me just taste it before you put it in," she said in between licks. She planted kisses on his eight inches, while eyeing it in admiration.

"Do whatever you like. We got all night."

He lightly placed his hand on top of her head. Jewel slurping the tip forced him to let out a snake like noise.

"Eat that dick," he mumbled, as he began to slowly thrust forward.

Boom! Boom! Boom!

Shots fired.

"Get down, Jewel," he yelled, alarmed. He quickly pulled up his clothes and ran downstairs.

Shaking like she'd just hit some bad dope, Jewel clutched the carpet underneath her as tears descended down her face. Blotchy caught up to the gang of men who were shooting dice and followed them out the front door towards the mayhem, guns drawn. Jewel quickly got dressed.

"Myesha," Jewel cried out. She repeatedly called her name in the midst of all the commotion. All she could hear was screaming, gun shots, and the shattering of glass.

Ssskkrry!

Suddenly, everything stopped. Panting, Jewel peered around nervously, still afraid to move.

"They trying to get away. Let's ride. We gon' follow these niggas!" She was sure the voice belonged to Blotchy, but she couldn't prove it

Jewel scurried to her feet and out of the room, down the stairs, and into Myesha's arms. The girls rocked side to side for what felt like forever. Sirens could be heard from a distance.

"We need to leave before they decide to come back," Jewel announced, grabbing Myesha's hand and rushing towards the front door.

"You good?" Jewel asked, drawing back and giving her a quick once over, as they stood on the other side of the door.

"Yeah, I'm good."

Jewel peered around, hoping she'd see either Blotchy or Big Dooski, but she spotted neither of them.

"They all rode out," Myesha mumbled, as she peered down at the grass. Guilt consumed her. It was her fault they were even there.

"Un-un, don't start. We got to find a way to Aunt Bey's."

The girls began footing it down the street. Police cruisers by-passed them.

"She's not going to let us in, Jewel, after a certain time," Myesha informed, while trying to keep up with Jewel.

"Really?" Jewel questioned in disbelief.

"Really," she assured.

Ah'Million

Chapter 16
Bobby

Bobby left Murder and Kad inside the studio, after being informed from someone employed with his security system that a possible break-in was taking place. The three of them had been in the studio for hours trying to successfully record his new song. Kad didn't believe in breaks or time off. He hated leaving business unfinished. Since Danielle passed, he focused more on work, unsure if he even grieved properly.

Poor Jewel. She'd lost one parent to the grave and the other to his career. Kad was simply steadfast on stacking paper and staying busy, a win-win situation, so he thought.

Police cruisers crowded the narrow street, making it difficult for Bobby to bypass. Groups of teens mobbed down the street on both sides. Bobby assumed that they all were party guests seeing how they were dressed. He swerved into the driveway of one of his properties. He climbed out hastily, ready to catch the intruders in action. His pace was quick, but the closer he got, it slowed.

Someone had been shooting. The window was shattered, and bullet holes decorated the front door, two bullets were still lodged in the door. Bobby unlocked the door and took a look inside. Seeing everything was fine, he stepped out on the porch and called Kad.

"Yo?" he answered.

"Nigga, somebody done shot my shit up." He stood at the curb, peering around at all the activity across the street. He wanted answers.

"The fuck? Just let me know how you want to play it."

"What the fuck?" Bobby mouthed, stunned.

"Let me call you back. The police walking towards me," he lied. Without giving Kad a chance to respond he ended the call.

"Jewel!"

Her head snapped in his direction. Realizing it was Bobby, she made a weak attempt of covering herself, but her hands simply weren't big enough for all the skin she had on display. The state of shock was evident, but it was too late to hide.

Kad don't know she's here, especially not dressed like this, Bobby thought. He saw everything she intended for the party guests to see. She was ashamed. He could tell by the way she dragged in his direction, her and Myesha. You would've thought they were going to a club, instead of a typical house party, by the way they were dressed.

"Are you going to tell my dad?" Jewel asked, avoiding eye contact. There was no denying that she looked stunning in the two-piece. The crop top accentuated her full breasts. The slit was a bit too revealing, but it was definitely sexy.

"I'm not a damn snitch. Y'all don't look harmed, so it's nothing to tell."

A slow smile spread across Jewel's face. She loved Bobby's *I don't give a fuck* attitude.

Although, inwardly he was a lil pissy. Kad was so uptight and overprotective that he refused to buy her a ride, which made no sense because she still found ways to do what she wanted to do. It actually made shit more difficult and dangerous. If she had her own ride, she wouldn't be standing around looking, half ass naked.

In spite of the way Bobby felt, he would never voice it. He remained neutral and detached towards anything or anyone that didn't pertain to him or his Big Momma. Inwardly, Bobby blamed Kad for his bid and the death of his father in the midst of it. He felt that if he would have never been sent away, he would've been there to say his goodbyes before his pop's time ran out. He may have never expressed to Kad how he felt, but there were vows he made to himself, before being released from prison.

Jewel and Myesha stood before him, stealing glances at one another, afraid to ask Bobby for a ride. Bobby deeply sighed, realizing what was going on.

"Come on. Where y'all headed?"

The three of them climbed inside the truck.

"Well, we supposed to be at Aunt Bey's," Jewel began.

"But, she's not going to let us in after a certain time. According to my time, we done already missed curfew," Myesha chimed in from the backseat.

"A little cash would make her change her mind," Jewel whispered.

Bobby shook his head in disgust. He knew Bey to be unstable and conniving, but he certainly wasn't expecting to hear that. Before dropping the girls off, he stopped at McDonalds to grab them a bite to eat. Occasionally, he would cut his eye at Jewel. Seeing the way she devoured her food indicated that she was high. Whatever dude she showed up with convinced her to smoke.

He came to a stop in front of Bey's apartments. "Give this to Bey." He slid two bills off the top.

"Thank you so much, Bobby. I don't know what I'd do without you." Jewel leaned over and wrapped her arms around his neck.

Her scent floated into his personal space, triggering shit he instantly rejected. The feel of her soft skin around his neck and pressed against his cheek was enough to arouse any man, homo or hetero.

"You good," he simply replied.

Her and Myesha climbed out of the truck and headed inside.

***

"Hey, lady," Bobby spoke. He planted a kiss on his grandmother's cheek and sat down.

"I made you an apple pie. It's wrapped up on top of the stove."

Bobby held her plump hand with his, as he gazed at her attentively.

"I just had breakfast, but I'm certainly going to take it with me."

Bobby loved his grandmother more than anything in the world. Seeing her age saddened him. He stroked her tousled gray hair, as he inwardly wished that she'd have just as many years in her as he had in him.

"How's life treating ya?" She peered over her glasses.

"I'm good, grandma, just enjoying your presence."

"How's Kad?"

Bobby had only revealed to his grandmother how he truly felt about Kad, and sure enough, she responded like most grandmothers would. "You can't blame no one but yourself. Forgive that boy, so God can forgive you, and move on with your life."

Bobby did just as his grandmother instructed, but there was no denying the bit of unforgiveness that lingered.

"He's good. We're about to meet up at the studio, once I leave here."

"Son, I've been meaning to tell you." She paused. "Don't be afraid, nor refuse, to let people in 'cause you don't want to end up loving them, which will summon your loyalty. Being loyal is simply in you, not on you, so just live and keep God close, just in case you find yourself in a situation you can't get out of."

Bobby looked at his seventy-two-year-old grandmother inquisitively. His grandmother never ceased to amaze him. Like many times before, he hadn't even given her the title of the book, yet she could summarize it entirely with just a few sentences.

"What made you say all of that, ma?"

The ringing of Bobby's phone diverted both of their attention.

"Hello?" The toll-free number was unfamiliar, but he answered anyways.

"You have a collect call from… Kadrick McVale."

***

After finding out Kad was arrested for sexual assault, Bobby immediately left his grandmother's and contacted his attorney, whom he kept on standby. Supposedly, the woman who claimed to be the victim was his current secretary, Susie. The day he hired the bitch, Bobby knew it was a mistake. Kad felt that since she wasn't his preferred race, he wouldn't fuck her like he'd done the others.

The tires screeched as Bobby stopped abruptly in front of the building. Just as expected, Susie was gone. Bobby examined everything attentively. Nothing was missing, except her things.

Fuck!

Bobby knew this meant he would have to step up, being that there was no Kad, nor secretary. He was used to playing the behind the scene position. He locked up the office and hurried back to his truck. The last person he wanted to break the news to was Jewel. He peered down at his screen and sneered in irritation. He quickly rejected Kesha's call, and phoned Jewel.

Ah'Million

Chapter 17
Jewel

Jewel didn't know if it was the cup of liquor she'd drank or the potent weed she'd inhaled that made her feel like shit the next day. She sat on the edge of Myesha's queen size bed, waiting for nothing in particular. She peered over her shoulder. Myesha's side of the bed was empty. She never really understood why she woke up so early.

"I need to shake this shit."

Jewel scooted off the bed and onto her feet. Her head felt so heavy, as if someone had placed their luggage on top of it. She struggled to pick up Myesha's bedroom door and place it against the wall. Bey was so elated to receive the two hundred dollars that she promised Myesha to put her door back. She gave it back, makeshift style, promising to properly screw it back in the morning.

Jewel dragged to the restroom and handled her hygiene before returning to the room.

"Hey, sleepy head," Myesha greeted with a smile big enough to light up the room.

"Where you been? All happy and shit, it's nine in the morning."

"I was in the living room watching TV. Besides, I'm used to getting up this early. That bitch don't let no one sleep late around here." She pointed towards her mother's room. "She just quiet for now, 'cause you here. That nigga probably in there." Myesha flopped down on her bed.

Jewel's eyes widened in concern. "She's going to make me leave?"

Myesha shook her head slowly. "Well, she usually stops tripping once she gets the nigga. As long as you in here, and not bouncing around the nigga, you good."

"It's her home girls and my sister she don't play about," Myesha continued.

Ring! Ring! Ring!

Jewel's head swiveled in the direction of her phone on Mye-sha's dresser. She scurried to it, sneering in confusion.

"Bobby," she whispered.

"Hello?"

"Get your things and come outside. I'm taking you home."

"Is everything alright?"

"I'll tell you in the car."

Concern consumed Jewel, instantly making her heart beat rapidly. She ended the call with Bobby and hastily gathered her things.

"Bobby is taking me home. I'll call you later. I love you." Jewel rushed towards the door with her handful of belongings.

"You okay?" Myesha called out from her door.

"Yeah, I'm going to call you." Jewel wasted no time descending the steps and climbing into Bobby's truck.

"Hey, Bobby. What's going on?" She searched his handsome face. Even in the state of concern, coupled with an ounce of fear, she still found him frightfully appeasing.

He looked at Jewel, then back at the road. He hated to be the bearer of bad news.

"Jew." He shortened her name, something he did seldomly. "Your dad's in the county on some bullshit charges. He should be out in a few days, if not tomorrow. I'm doing everything I can."

"What?" she shrieked.

Immediately the floodgates opened, and she began to sob like a child.

"I can't believe this! My mother, now this?" she looked up towards the ceiling as if she was talking to the Almighty. "No, no. Uh-un, I can't do this. What if they don't let him out? What I'm gon' do, Bobby?" She peered at him, Hopeless and helpless. Her lips quivered as tears fell down her face rapidly.

Seeing Jewel so discouraged troubled him deeply. She was innocent, and too beautiful to be met with some of the ugliest circumstances she'd been faced with. Bobby pulled over at the nearest gas station.

"Come here, Jew."

She leaned over into his arms, wailing harder than she'd done previously.

"Stop crying. I'm gon' get him out of there. And always know, if you don't have no one, you have me," Bobby promised, holding her tightly as he slightly rocked her back and forth.

Secretly she wished she could stay there forever. Once the tears let up, Bobby released his hold and proceeded to her house, in silence.

"Call me if you need anything," he instructed, before pulling out of the driveway.

Jewel simply nodded. She didn't have the strength to do anything else.

Blotchy, on the other hand, had been calling Jewel non-stop, trying to apologize for vanishing the night before. He was hoping Kad would be at his office and he could just pop up on her for a few minutes. But after carelessly scrolling down his newsfeed on IG, he discovered something even better.

Fuck a few minutes, I'ma have all night, he thought, smirking mischievously.

"Aye, bruh, I'm gon' fuck with you later."

Big Dooski closed the top on the Big Peach he had been drinking. "Where you going?"

Blotchy walked from the rear of the store and stood on the opposite side of the counter, facing Big Dooski. "I'm about to go fuck with Jewel for a few hours," he admitted.

He and Big Dooski shared a similar grin as the bell sounded.

"I hope she on her grown woman, 'cause her girl still ain't let a nigga beat."

Blotchy could've sworn Dooski hit. Lil mama acted just like a hot girl, but looks can be deceiving. Instead of responding, he sneered in confusion. He looked from Big Dooski to the chick who'd just walked in.

"This you?" Blotchy asked curiously.

"Yeah, for the night."

***

After giving Blotchy the okay to come over, Jewel dragged herself out of the bed and took care of her hygiene. She was in no mood to apply any makeup. Although she really liked Blotchy and wanted badly to impress him, she simply did not have the strength. All she wanted was company to help her ease the pain of missing her father.

She carefully applied her mink lashes and began straightening up her room. Seeing her phone light up out of the corner of her eye, she quickly retrieved it. It was a text from Blotchy.

I'm outside.

Her heart began to race as she swiftly applied any finishing touches. She jogged to the door, not wanting to keep him waiting.

"Hey." She smiled faintly.

"Aww, come here, girl, you gon' be alright." Blotchy reached in and wrapped his arms around her small waist. His dick twitched as soon as her honey and vanilla scent assaulted his nostril.

"Damn, you smell good," he murmured into the crease of her neck. He smelled just as delicious. His Dylan Blue Versace fragrance aroused her. She led him inside, and they both sat on the sofa.

"Oh, I see you read," Blotchy said, picking up the urban novel.

"Hmmm, *Toe Tagz Show: No Love*. It got a nice ring to it." He looked at the synopsis on the back.

"It's actually a good book. It's some young niggas in there wildin', but it's a female as well, and she roguish, too."

Blotchy placed the book back on the table and turned to face Jewel. "Look, I punched on a nigga the other day, and he shot up my aunt's house in return." He paused. "I left because we went to go find them niggas, but there was no luck with that," he confessed.

"So, the big house where we were partying is your aunt's house?"

He nodded in agreement. "I'm sorry for leaving you, Jewel. I came back but saw the law and kept going. We had too many straps in the car to risk getting searched."

"I mean, we made it home just fine."

"You know what I'm really mad about?"

"What's that?"

"As soon as the shit really start feeling good, them niggas start bussin'." They both erupted in laughter. Jewel turned on a movie, then snuggled closer. Neither of them seemed too interested in the movie, as they continued to engage in conversation.

"Hold on." Jewel hopped up and dashed towards the kitchen.

Seeing the way her fat ass swallowed the booty shorts made Blotchy grit his teeth. She returned shortly with sodas, but the only thing he wanted to guzzle was her cum.

"You not thirsty?" She asked, once he placed his soda on the table.

"Not really."

Jewel took a small sip and sat hers down beside his. This time when she snuggled closer, his hands roamed her soft skin. He was tired of waiting. He slid his hand up her shorts and found her kitty.

She moaned.

He slid one finger between her moist slit and grazed her button.

"Oooh."

Bingo!

He made slow circles around her clit.

Jewel jerked at the feeling of the newfound pleasure. He sped up. A warm tingly feeling in her toes made her whimper like a hungry kitten. He slowed down, but applied more pressure.

"Oooh shit." Her head tilted back in pleasure. The feeling was unimaginable, so unreal that she closed her eyes, afraid she'd open them, and he'd be gone, along with the pleasure.

"I'm cumming!"

Her muscles contracted, her body shook, then she exploded. Her juices emerged from her tunnel, nearly coating Blotchy's entire hand. Jewel lay back breathlessly.

Smoothly and swiftly, he slid out of his briefs and jeans. The taste of her honey gave him an itch that he just had to scratch. He tossed the pillows off the sofa.

"Turn around and toot that ass up." He spoke with authority as he hovered over her, with his pole stretched to capacity.

Jewel did just as he instructed, putting her head down and against the crease of the couch. He stroked his dick in anticipation. He used his knee to spread her legs further, and pressed down on her back to give it more of an arch.

Once she was positioned to his liking, he knocked at her opening. Fear consumed Jewel immediately at the feel of his tip. He glided his thickness up and down her opening, then slowly eased the tip in.

She gasped.

He thrusted forward.

"Aaaaghh," she yelped out in pain as he tore through her flesh.

A hump formed in her back as she clenched her ass cheeks. With his dick still inside of her, Blotchy eased her back into the position she was in. He stroked her slowly but roughly. Pleasure surpassed the pain, and moans filled the room.

Slap!

"Throw it back," he demanded, slapping her ass twice more.

She attempted, but it was a weak attempt.

He grabbed a hold to her waist and stroked her kitty until he felt himself about to explode.

"Turn around."

Slowly and exhaustedly she did so.

He gripped the back of her head, pulled her closer, and shot his cum down her throat. Grunts filled the room. Jewel peered up in disgust at the foul taste of his warm liquid. He slowly removed his pole, and she kept it against her checks, afraid to swallow it.

"See, you still a kid. You don't even swallow the nut."

As quickly as the words left his tongue, the nut went down her throat. She was willing to do whatever just so he'd see her in a different light.

Chapter 18
Myesha

His shifty eyes revealed his evil intentions. He grew bolder as the days passed. He didn't cut his eyes, nor did he glance seldomly. He boldly watched Myesha as she walked to the refrigerator and back to her room, admiring her backside. Something was up. Bey didn't miss a beat, and surely, she didn't miss that.

Myesha closed the door to her bedroom and lay back on her bed. She had tried calling Jewel numerous times, but got her voicemail. She'd texted Big Dooski nearly an hour ago, yet it still hadn't been read. She smacked her lips and rolled over on her side. An hour or so had passed, and the sound of her door creaking abruptly awoke Myesha.

She lay facing her wall, with one eye open. Footsteps approached while everything else seemed to have ceased, including her breathing and beating heart. She spun around quickly, ready to face her fears. She squinted to make out the figure that stood motionless next to her dresser. Hardly any light seeped in from the living room, and without a TV of her own, and her phone lying face down, there wasn't a glimpse of light in her room.

"Myesha." Her mother flicked her light switch. Bey stood before her, crossing her arms over her chest.

"Ma'am?" Myesha clutched her chest, where her heart was located, in relief. She could've sworn it was her perverted as boyfriend, about to jack his dick, like she had caught him doing a few nights ago.

"Cut that innocent shit, bitch," Bey flipped out.

"Momma, what? What you-?"

"Shut the hell up! If you wouldn't be prancing your lil fast ass around here, I wouldn't be going through this."

Myesha was lost. It was as if her mother was speaking in riddles.

"What are you talking about?"

"All this motherfucker do is talk about you. I get sick of hearing about you." She pointed towards the living room, where he sat.

Fear pervaded through Myesha instantly. One thing her mother didn't play about was her bread. Myesha held her hands up in surrender, as she backed up closer to the wall.

"Ma, I don't have anything to do with that. He's sick!"

Myesha searched her mother's eyes, but she could tell by her tousled hair and vacant eyes that anything coming out her mouth would fall on deaf ears. Tears fell slowly. She had a premonition that something was about to happen that she wouldn't agree with. Bey chuckled, appearing to be in some sort of trance.

"You don't have nothing to do with it?"

Although she asked, it sounded more like a statement, making Myesha afraid to answer.

"Look, since this nigga don't want my pussy, you gone give him yours. You gon' satisfy him!"

A look of disbelief etched across Myesha's face. She couldn't believe her ears.

"You don't have to look appalled. I'm serious." She paused. "You gon' either fuck him or get the fuck out."

Myesha sighed deeply, lowering her head in disappointment. "I'll go," she spoke, lacking certainty, hoping Bey would change her mind in fear of her baby girl facing the mean streets of Dallas on her own. Yet she said nothing.

Myesha picked up her book bag and began tossing things inside.

"Un-un, since you leaving, don't take nothing my money bought."

Myesha squinted over her shoulder at her mother, awestruck. "For real, momma? You gon' put me out naked? With nothing to help me fend for myself?" This hurt surpassed any hurt Myesha had ever felt in her seventeen years on earth.

"You damn right, 'cause you shouldn't be trying to leave." She spoke calmly, as if she was voicing things that made sense.

"So, I should stay and let this old ass nigga fuck me? I'm a virgin, momma," she shrieked, then sobbed inside her palm of her hands. "My virginity is sacred to me," Myesha yelled in between sniffles.

Bey stood there smirking, as if Myesha was simply capping. Any remorse vanished the second it appeared. Coupled with agony, was shame, as Myesha flew past her mother.

"Be ready when you come back!" A sinister laugh erupted immediately afterwards.

Myesha flew out of the house and into the darkness. The same darkness the Bible speaks of, the one full of evil, impurity, wickedness, and corruption.

Who would take me in with nothing? Jewel was the first person who had come to her mind, but she realized she left her phone. The smoke shop didn't close until midnight. She could at least spend a night with Dooski and get dropped off at Jewel's in the morning.

Myesha flew down the steps and out of the apartment. She sprinted down the street as if someone was chasing her. That someone was her life. A life so foul she considered ending it because running from it seem merely temporary. She hopped over a small pool of water. Myesha looked like a track star jumping hurdles. She slowed her pace and bent the corner breathlessly, making her way inside the shopping mart.

A vacant lot, minus the car parked in front of the laundromat, and Dooski's outside the smoke shop. A deep sigh of relief escaped Myesha's mouth. She dusted off any residue from her clothing, so that she could appear normal once face to face with Dooski.

The door to the smoke shop opened and for a minute everything slowed down. A chick emerged from the store. Big Dooski slapped her on the ass before turning around to lock the store up. The thick brown skinned chick locked eyes with Myesha, only for a second, before she sprinted towards the direction she had come.

A wave of sorrow passed through Myesha, making her lose her balance and fall on one knee. The brown skinned chick sneered in confusion, while pointing at the spot where she had saw Myesha.

"What?" Dooski asked, looking off into the distance in the direction she pointed.

Not wanting to kill his vibe, she tore her eyes from the now vacant spot. "Nothing. I'm tripping."

Dooski shrugged, then slid inside his car, anxious to slide in something else.

As eager as Myesha was to find Big Dooski, she wasn't as eager to return home. Her shoulders sagged and her feet dragged while in pursuit to the Devil's lair. The glimmer of hope she had ten minutes ago was gone, like a candle that had been blown out.

Left with no choice but one, Myesha returned home shortly. She surrendered to any and all commands and let her mother's boyfriend have his way with her.

Myesha awoke the next morning, feeling like she had been in a car wreck the previous night. The monstrous migraine made it difficult for her to open her eyes, and the soreness between her legs confined her to the bed. Sunlight seeped through her tattered blinds.

I have to go to school, she thought.

It was too late for that. School started two hours ago. Finally, Myesha found strength to lift up onto her elbows. The sight of the dry blood that stained her thighs caused her to faint. She fell into a deep slumber again.

***

"Hey girlie," Jewel spoke as soon as she entered Myesha's room.

Myesha smiled faintly, sitting on her bed with her knees pulled into her chest.

"What's wrong?" She dropped her MCM bag and rushed to her side.

"I'm good. I just got a bad headache and my body a lil sore."

"Aww, hell nah! Where my mask? Bitch, them COVID symptoms."

If only she knew, Myesha thought with a chuckle, then rolled her eyes.

"Well, I brought this to make you feel better." Jewel tossed the Ziploc bag on her lap with a few cigarillos.

Myesha sneered up at her in confusion.

"What? You too fucked up to roll up?" Jewel asked.

"Nah." She paused. "I'm just shocked you got all of it without the help of me, little miss sweet and innocent."

Laughter filled the room. Jewel removed her shoes and sat next to Myesha on the bed. In spite of the window being ajar, purple haze instantly crammed the small room. Jewel rambled to Myesha about everything going on with her father. Myesha listened attentively, although she wanted badly to recall last night's events. If she was going to tell anyone, it would be Jewel but a part of her felt too humiliated to do that.

"Girl, I knew I had something to tell you." Jewel paused, hitting the weed. "I lost my virginity."

Myesha gasped, nearly choking on the smoke. *That makes two of us*, she thought.

"The day my dad got arrested, Blotchy came over. It was so good. I been fiending for more."

Inwardly, Myesha always wished her first time would be something she'd always remember, but now she wished like hell she could soon forget it. She listened to Jewel ceaselessly talk highly about Blotchy's sex game, as she drifted into her own thoughts. Hearing about Blotchy only made her hate Dooski more.

"Have you talked to him?" Myesha asked.

"No, but I texted him when I got out of school and asked him to pull up."

Ah'Million

Chapter 19
Kad

"Aye, that's me," Kad said to the bulky Hispanic dude. His head was bald as a goose egg and mediocre tattoos covered his face. Kad stood to his feet.

"I'm dialing again, homes. She didn't answer."

Kad pinched the bridge of his nose before sitting back down. *This nigga done dialed like ten times already,* he thought.

This was only day four, but it felt like day forty. Today he would finally be given the chance to go to magistrate court and get a bond. Because he came on a Friday, and it was already extremely late by the time he booked in, he wasn't allowed to see the judge until today.

He couldn't believe Susie played the game so raw and uncut, as if he was some type of Chester the Molester ass nigga. Even though she didn't initiate it, she did the furthest thing from stopping it, indicating that she wanted it just as bad as he did.

He had never been so anxious to see a judge, even though he was scared as shit. Susie coming forth was probable but finding out that Tisha had done so, too, was far-fetched. Her *"me-too"* ass had hopped on the bandwagon. Yet, in all actuality, she was a hurt bitch. Two charges still shouldn't have been enough to deny Kad bond, when he'd never had a run-in with the law.

"Aye, homes." The Hispanic dude held the phone out for Kad to grab. Finally.

He retrieved the phone and dialed Bobby's number.

"Yo," he answered.

"What it's looking like?"

"Everything good, fam. We all in the lobby, waiting for court to begin, the attorney, me, Sierra, and Jewel. Sierra's presence surprised him indeed.

"Okay, Okay."

"Yeah, don't trip, you good. Hold on."

"Hey, dad, I love you."

"I love you, too, baby girl."

"McVale!"

Kad looked back to see the C.O. standing at the door.

"Come on. You got court."

Kad said his goodbyes and quickly ended the call. He shot a silent prayer up to the heavens on his way to the courtroom. Immediately, he met the face of his two favorite people, as soon as they led him inside.

"The state of Texas vs Kadrick McVale."

Bobby watched how his attorney spoke swiftly and effortlessly, making Kad sound like more of a victim than the suspect. She took a seat as the judge sifted through the paperwork in front of him.

"Kadrick McVale, bond sat at 100,000 dollars."

Before the judge could bang his gavel, the prosecutor objected. Every head in the courtroom tuned in his direction.

"I was just notified of this new evidence you might find interesting, regarding Mr. McVale's bond."

Kad's heart began to beat rapidly as he swiftly considered anything additional that would jeopardize his freedom. The prosecutor placed the disk inside the DVD player. It was a phone call. He fast forward the call to the part that needed to be heard. Kad instantly realized the two voices belonged to him and Sierra.

"I get out this bitch, they gon' have to catch me in Dubai. I be damn if I sit around and let them ho's Bill Cosby me."

Gasp filled the room. The prosecutor played it a second time, and Kad dropped his head in defeat. The judge immediately revoked his bond, labeling him a flight risk.

"Hell nah!" Bobby stood to his feet.

"I love you, dad," Jewel blurted before burying her face into her hands, sobbing.

"I got you, zaddy," Sierra promised.

Kad was so enraged that he could have cried. He had a feeling that this was going to be the beginning of some bullshit.

Chapter 20
Bobby

"Bobby, I'm pregnant." Those three words had tainted Bobby's mind since the day Kesha spoke them. He yearned to give his grandmother a grandchild, especially before it was too late, but Kesha simply didn't meet the criteria.

She was weak, lacked ambition, and was always trying to count everyone else's bag but her own. Bobby sat in his truck waiting for her to emerge from the house. He knew there was a multitude of foul possibilities, but he didn't speak on it. Mainly because it was a probable possibility that he could be the father. *Why fuss over a problem that can be removed?* He thought.

Kesha finally emerged from her condo. There was no denying her sex appeal. She was stacked, beautiful in the face, with a walk that demanded everyone's attention. None of it moved Bobby. She was still as replaceable as a bald head bitch with no ass.

She climbed into the truck. Bobby could tell by the mug on her face she was upset. If she thought for one minute that he trusted her with his bread, she was sadly mistaken. Bobby wasn't the type to pop up and make his chick piss on a stick. He felt that if she was playing games, she was only playing herself. A couple hundred for a mishap was fine with him because he surely wouldn't make the same mistake twice.

"Good morning." He peeled out of the lot.

Kesha eyed him menacingly, sneering in disbelief. "So, you want a bitch to be jolly. Jolly, after what I'm about to go do?"

Kesha desperately wanted to keep the baby but knowing how much it would upset Bobby made her opt against it. Doing the opposite of what he desired would surely upset him to the point of unforgiveness. The last thing she wanted was for Bobby to walk away completely.

Hearing her smart remark, he shook his head and turned the volume on his music to the max. Like a child throwing a tantrum, she flopped against the seat, pouting the rest of the ride to the clinic.

"Hey," she tapped him on the shoulder.

Bobby turned the music down.

"Stop up there at that first clinic on the left. I have to speak with my doctor first."

Bobby veered into the lot.

Kesha rushed inside. "I don't have an appointment, but I'm here to see Dr. Shells."

"She's with someone right now, but I'll let her know once she's done," the receptionist replied.

"Okay, thank you."

Kesha found an empty seat and sat down. She turned her nose up in disgust at the family that sat a few feet away from her. She pulled out her tube of gloss and applied it to her full lips. Their impoverished presence made her skin crawl. Kesha tore her eyes from the children upon spotting a teenage girl emerge from the back teary eyed. She didn't have knowledge of her current situation, but her terror-stricken expression was one she was indeed familiar with.

"Ma'am," Dr. Shells yelled from the entryway.

The girl turned around at the sound of her voice.

"I have to give you your prescription."

STD, Kesha thought. The young chick lowered her head in shame as she went to retrieve the piece of paper from Dr. Shells.

We all go through that, baby girl. Don't be like me. Take this as a lesson learned and quit letting them niggas go dirty dick dancing in yah' shit. She instantly felt pity for the young chick. She reminded Kesha a lot of herself. *A young cutie with a booty.*

It was hard shying from men, who wanted nothing but her goodies, when her assets made her the center of attention. Unfortunately, it took years to decipher the difference between lust and love.

Bobby sat outside in his truck, waiting patiently, when Jewel hastily emerged from the clinic. She was moving so fast she didn't even see him. The hoodie was a lame attempt at concealing her identity because he spotted her effortlessly. He hadn't really spoken to Jewel since court. Bobby bit down on his lip to refrain from yelling her name. That cape was taken off years ago. He couldn't allow other people's problems to become his.

If she was really into some shit, she would call.

He tore his eyes from Jewel and the yearning to protect her that tugged at his heart strings. There was no way he was going to allow someone else's burdens to force him to think irrationally and take a loss. He couldn't afford to lose anything else. He had already lost so much.

Ah'Million

Chapter 21
Jewel

"He burnt me," Jewel wailed. She buried her head into Myesha's chest, as she slowly rocked her back and forth. Her chest heaved uncontrollably, as her tears soaked Myesha's shirt.

"It's gon' be okay. Just take your pill and it'll be gone. You not the first female with a STD, and surely won't be the last."

Since her father's first court appearance, another female had come forth. It was now a total of three. With the absence of her father and betrayal from her dude, Jewel needed a vacation. She needed to go anyplace but her own. She packed two overnight bags and went to her Aunt Bey's.

Bey knew something was wrong with Jewel, sensing her gloomy mood, but she assumed it was something dealing with her father's situation.

"Don't be sad, niece. They lying on my brother. Look how they doing R. Kelly! I don't give a shit. Fuck iTunes, I'm gon' jam him til' the day I die." She walked out, singing the twelve play lyrics.

Blotchy had tried calling Jewel, but it was Myesha who sent him to voicemail every time. In spite of Blotchy's obscenity, Jewel could not shake him from her mind. Any form of apology would give them normalcy again. She was hurt, but only he could heal her.

After a few blunts, Myesha had fallen asleep, and Jewel snuck off to phone Blotchy.

He answered on the first ring. "Hello? Damn, where you been? Nigga outchea going through it, and you don't even give a damn."

"What are you talking about? I'm going-"

"Nigga robbed me, and almost put me to sleep on top of that!" He chimed in, ceasing her speech.

"Where you at? I'm about to come get you and tell you all about it."

"I'm at Myesha's," she blurted before thinking.

Perhaps it would be a good thing, and they could talk face to face. She ended the call quickly and rushed back inside to prep for an evening with Blotchy. She thought of several ways to approach Blotchy, as the hot water descended down her back. She wanted answers, the most justifiable excuse he could think of, along with a sincere apology. By the time Jewel was done and ready to go, Aunt Bey had returned.

"Hey, niecy." She waved from the sofa.

"Here, aunty. I'll be back in like three hours." She handed Bey a seventh of Kush and fifty bucks. Bey's face lit up like a kid on Christmas Day.

"Oooh shit!" She held up the bag and rattled it.

Jewel slid out and down the stairs. The weather was fair, as the sun began to set. Dudes crowded the breezeway, spitting weak game. The bass from Blotchy's G-wagon almost shook the slab beneath her feet. As soon as they locked eyes, her heart melted. She had managed to forget about her whole visit to the clinic.

"Hey, lady," he greeted, as soon as she slammed the door shut.

Before she could respond, he leaned over and planted a slow, wet kiss on her lips. The drive to the studio was quiet, except for Blotchy's phone call. Things seemed pretty explosive in the beginning but toned down by the time they entered the lot of the studio. Jewel seemed pretty concerned, but feared voicing them. He grabbed her by the hand, leading her inside and through the studio.

Jewel sneered in confusion as she treaded over objects in front of her. It looked like they had a big celebration the night before, and no one bothered to clean up.

Seeing her reaction, Blotchy quickly said, "Excuse the mess, my lil bro got out last night."

"Um, I wasn't invited to the party?"

"Nah, bae, stripper hoes only."

Blotchy's comment offended Jewel like an unexpected foul odor.

"Damn, that was disrespectful."

"Nah, it was the truth." He tossed his letterman's jacket on the arm of sofa, flopped down, then pulled Jewel down on top of him. "Fuck what you talking about, I'm trying to disrespect that lil' pussy between your legs."

Jewel was so attracted to his vulgar speech. That slick mouth of his made her pussy wet. She feared ruining the moment with telling him about the STD. So, she opted against it. Initially, she hoped they'd eat, chat, sex, and then chill, but so much for wishful thinking.

Blotchy effortlessly finessed her out of her clothes and fucked her raw until he came twice. Knowing his dick was dirtier than a prostitute's leggings, she still let him bounce in and out of her walls, contaminating her pussy even more.

***

"Niecy, you gotta be the slowest bitch on Earth."

Jewel glanced up at her aunty in shame. Myesha was asleep when she made it back, so she vented to her aunt instead.

"I just didn't know how to tell him." Her eyes remained glued to the floor. She was too ashamed to look her aunt in the eyes.

"The hell you mean *scared*? Scared of who? You only get one pussy! You young, beautiful, and smart. He fuck around and give you something incurable and fuck up your whole future."

A pool of tears welled in Jewel's eyes, threatening to fall at any second. Although her and Blotchy's relationship was brief, she didn't want anyone but him. She knew he wouldn't intentionally hurt her, and she definitely didn't want to offend him.

"How can I get by without telling him?"

"Tuh." Bey shook her head in disgrace.

"Tell him you on your period. Take your medicine. It takes seven days to work, but you can't have sex. The only thing is, you'll risk getting it again if he's still infected."

Ah'Million

Chapter 22
Bobby

Bobby sat on the opposite side of the glass, visiting his childhood friend. The weight loss was a sure indication of stress. He went from one to three of the same charges in less than a week. On top of all that, he had to stay incarcerated and fight the bullshit. Kad was many things, but a perv, he wasn't. He had always been a ladies' man. Bagging a broad was an effortless task for both Kad and Bobby.

"I'm just glad Sierra sided with a nigga, instead of against me. Shit, I'd have four fucking charges."

"You right about that. Do you want something out of the vending machine before my time up?" Although a piece of him blamed Kad for his incarceration, he truly felt sorry for him.

"I'm good, Bobby. I don't even have an appetite."

Bobby leaned closer. "Look, just chill. You gon' be straight. You got the best lawyer money can buy. And if these hoes want hush money, we gon' give it to 'em."

Bobby left, giving Kad more hope in his situation. He wanted badly to express his concern for Jewel, but he didn't want to add to the stress. He left the jail and headed for Kad's. He pulled up into the driveway shortly thereafter. He was ready to spazz and kick the door in when his knocks went unanswered, but decided to call her before doing so.

"You home, Jewel?"

"No, I had to get away. I'm at aunt Bey's."

"Are you good? Do you need anything?"

"I'm low on money, Bobby, that's it."

Hearing her tone of voice bothered Bobby. "Okay, I got you." He ended the call quickly. But instead of going to Bey's, which he dreaded, he texted her and asked her for her CashApp instead. A beautiful woman in distress weakened the strongest men. He wouldn't allow Jewel's problems to become his own, and to succeed at that would mean keeping his distance.

***

"So, Kemp, what happen to my shit?"

Kemp and Bobby sat behind tint in his ride. There were too many ears inside the small barbershop, so they found privacy in Kemp's tricked out Cadillac Deville. Kemp was an old school that had been in the mix for years. He knew everyone of importance, whether they had new money, old money, a little money, or a lot.

"Supposedly, it's some beef going on, North Dallas versus the Cliff." He sucked his teeth. Kemp was a dark skin brother with a mouth full of golds. "Blotchy had a bad run in at his store with one of them guys from the *Nawf.* Beat him up real bad, I heard."

"When was this?" Bobby listened attentively.

The old man had just confirmed his suspicion. Blotchy had lied to Kad about not being involved in street beef.

"I'm not for sure. Well, Blotchy threw a party recently and ol' boy shot the place up. Blotchy and his boys buss'd back. I didn't hear anything about anyone getting hurt."

They must've hit my shit trying to hit their target, Bobby thought. "So that spot where they had the party is Blotchy's?" Bobby was eager to know more about this cat, especially since he was soon to become a member of the squad.

"Nah, it's his aunt's. Older lady, she attends church missions for months at a time." He paused. "He keeps an eye on the place for her."

"Okay, okay." Bobby rubbed his goatee as he began to calculate his next move.

"Just swing by if you need me. I hope these young niggas haven't tore my shit up! These new millennium kids so damn throwed, you'd think they came from another planet."

They shared a laugh. Kemp opened the car door. He placed one foot outside of the car then looked back at Bobby before getting out.

"Youngsta was just trying to defend himself. You nor your spot was the target. It's not even worth you getting worked up behind." He slid out and disappeared into his shop.

Kemp was right there was no need to act out or violent. It was a simple mistake.

***

"Hey, ma, Bobby called out from the front door, shutting the door behind him. Worry lines etched his forehead as he made his way through the house.

"Ma?"

"I'm in the tub."

Bobby rushed inside. Her warm smile instantly calmed his fears. Deeply sighing, he let down the toilet seat and sat down.

"Ma, you scared me."

"Scared you? Bobby, it's nothing to be afraid of. Sugar."

He tore his eyes from her and shook his head slowly.

"Don't worry 'bout me. With the God I serve, just hope I don't outlive you."

"I believe I'd prefer it that way."

She went on with her bath as if Bobby wasn't sitting there. "You forgot, didn't you?"

"Forgot what?"

"Today I have a doctor's appointment."

He grabbed both sides of his head. "Aww, shoot, that's right." He stood to leave. "I'll be waiting in the living room."

***

"Excuse me. Let me give you two some privacy." The nurse eased around Bobby and walked out.

He swiveled around, his eyes lingered on her backside.

"Get yo manish 'hind over here."

Bobby chuckled. "Ma, what you talking about?" He couldn't hide his grin.

"That woman could be married."

The last thing Bobby wanted to hear was a sermon. "Is she getting all the paperwork together?"

"Yes and no. I have to stay another night."

His heart beat feverishly. He grabbed ahold of the railing. "What do you mean another night?"

There it was again, that smile of hers that was so soothing. "Boy, calm down. Per protocol, if you over the age of sixty-five, they test you for COVID. You're hospitalized until your results come back."

Bobby deeply sighed. "Oh, okay. I'm good, ma!" He sat down on the loveseat next to the bed, reclined back, and zipped up his Amiri hoodie.

"Boy, what are you doing?"

"Getting comfortable. When they release you, we'll leave together."

"Child, visiting hours are over."

The nurse walked in. "In an hour. Visitation is from 11am to 4pm.

"Preciate you, I'll stay until then."

"Ms. Taylor, dinner is being prepped and it'll be served short-ly."

"Thank you, nurse."

The nurse disappeared again, and Bobby made sure he kept his eyes low. He stayed with his grandmother another hour and promised to visit the next day.

Chapter 23
Myesha

"I'm going to hop in the shower real quick." Jewel dropped her handbag on the table and darted to the restroom.

Tonight would be Myesha's first time seeing Big Dooski since the night she saw him leaving the store with a chick, but she was anxious to see him. Bey had been oddly quiet since Jewel was practically paying her to stay there.

"She been fucking."

Hearing her mother's voice, Myesha stopped in her tracks and hid behind the wall. She was sure she was talking on the phone because the only voice she heard was her mother's.

"Ain't nobody staying in my house for free. That's why Brandi and Bianca got the fuck up outta here!"

Who is she talking to? Myesha wondered.

"That, or I'll take it out of her ass." She chuckled.

Anger coupled with disbelief consumed Myesha and she retreated to her room.

***

"This is good," Jewel commented, sucking her fingers.

The four of them enjoyed their evening at Red Lobster, despite the tension. Conversation was minimal between Myesha and Dooski. Jewel noticed something wasn't right when she saw that she hadn't touched her food.

"Have you talked to your dad recently?" Blotchy asked, draping his arm over Jewel's shoulder.

"I don't really want to talk about it, bae. Can we talk about it later?"

"Cool."

Jewel leaned up and planted a kiss on his lips.

Cling! The sound of the fork hitting the plate grabbed all of their attention.

"Come on, Myesha, let me holla at you outside real quick."

121

Myesha peered up at him anxiously.

"Come on." His tone brooked no argument.

She stood and followed him out of the restaurant and into the wintriness. Once outside of the restaurant, Big Dooski turned around and wrapped Myesha into a tight hug.

"You cold?"

"Mm-hmmm," she nodded.

"What's wrong, bae? Talk to me, I miss you."

Myesha leaned back to look into his eyes. "You love her?"

He released his grip. "Love who?" His eyes were the size of golf balls.

"The girl I saw you leaving the store with that night."

His mouth hung open as he thought hard on the woman she was referring to. "Really, love? I hit that bitch that night and that was it. If she wanted some dick again, she couldn't get none 'cause we didn't even exchange numbers. Wait." He paused. "Is this what you in your feelings about?"

Myesha swiped the tears from her eyes.

He grabbed her face with both of his massive hands. "Baby girl, I know you a virgin and yo' virginity is sacred. Since we been fucking around, I haven't pressed you once." He paused. "But you have to understand, I'm a man with needs. I just get my dick wet from time to time, but all I want is you. I'm not stut'n these hoes."

Tears raced rapidly down Myesha's face uncontrollably, but it wasn't because of his passionate speech. Guilt was eating Myesha up. She was keeping something from a man who pulled at her heart strings, but giving that exact same thing to a man she despised wholeheartedly.

"I have something to tell you."

Meanwhile, inside the restaurant…

"I can't do that, Blotchy."

"Bruh, your dad isn't getting out right now with those odds against him." He moved his hands frantically. "The only thing that's going to keep him from getting a lot of time, is money. A lot of it. What you gon' do then?"

"I don't want to think about that," she buried her face into her palms.

"Stop crying." He grabbed her hands, moving them from her tear stained face. "Look, baby girl, you can't count no one else money but, yours. Remember that."

***

"Damn, girl, about time you wake up," Myesha said, while cleaning out her drawer.

"I'm trying to sleep late as I can. Come tomorrow, I can't." She raised up.

"Yeah, if you need a ride to school, I can have Big Dooski pick you up."

Jewel stared at her curiously. "What you mean?"

Myesha stopped cleaning and turned around. "Jewel, I'm leaving tomorrow, and I'm not coming back."

"Wha-what?" She jumped out of bed.

"I'm going to stay with Big Dooski, and you're going back home. This bitch not right." She pointed towards her mother's room. "I'll be damned if I leave you here."

"It, it's just so sudden."

"You don't know the half of it." She paused, tearing her eyes from Jewel. "She don't want me here anyways. It's about time I give her what she wants."

After several attempts, and getting just a voicemail, Jewel phoned Bobby to pick her up.

Ah'Million

Chapter 24
Bobby

It was ten minutes after eleven. Once Bobby scooped Jewel, he planned to be at the hospital by twelve to see his grandmother, with hopes of taking her home. Detecting her gloomy mood, Bobby turned the music down.

"Bad night?"

Jewel tore her eyes from the scenery on the other side of the window and looked at him. She deeply sighed. "Well, Myesha is moving out." She paused. "I'm a little upset because I know it won't be the same."

Inwardly, Bobby was curious to know more details dealing with the move, but he refused to expose his concerns. "Damn, well at least y'all will see each other at school."

"Yeah, I guess that's good enough." She paused. "Do you think you can drop me off at school?"

"What time you have to be there?"

"Eight."

He tightened his lips. "Well I—"

"You don't have to. I was just asking if you could."

"See, I got a meeting at seven with an investor. Then, at 8:15, I have to meet up with this journalist, who wants to interview Murder." He smacked his lips. "It's no way I'll make it on time."

"Ok. I'll just ask-"

"Y'all spot is a good distance from the office."

"Well, where do you stay?"

Bobby locked eyes with Jewel. Silence filled the car.

She chuckled nervously. "Okay, how far do you stay from the office?"

"Ten minutes." *Chill, Bobby, everyone isn't out to get you,* he mentally reassured himself.

"Well, can I spend the night at your house?"

The question most definitely startled Bobby, as he swallowed the lump in his throat.

"Yeah, I don't see why not. You need to stop by your spot to get some stuff?"

"Yeah."

Within minutes, Bobby pulled up to the house she shared with her father. It took her only a minute to gather some things, and they were back on the road.

"Look, make yourself comfortable. I'll be back in a few hours. I have some business to tend to," he said, removing the key from the chain of keys.

***

Bobby eased inside his grandmother's room, exposing his pearly whites. He hid the Williams chicken behind his back as he walked closer to her bed.

She's asleep, he said to himself.

He sat the chicken down on the stand next to the loveseat. "Ma?" He called out. "Hey, Ma, wake up. It's time to go." Panic pervaded through him, seeing that she wasn't budging. He rubbed her arm softly. "Ma?" His brows dipped in confusion.

Maybe she's just on some type of anesthesia, he thought. He rushed towards the door, as the nurse entered.

"Oooh, shit. Hey, I-I'm sorry. I almost-"

Bobby cut her off. "It's cool. Look, what's wrong with my grandma? Why isn't she waking up?"

"She slipped into a Diabetic coma last night."

His chest tightened. He leaned against the wall for leverage. "A diabetic coma?" He whispered. "Wh'what happened? I take good care of her. I make sure she has taken her insulin and I monitor what she eats." He searched her face swiftly.

"She was supposed to have told you last night, but sir, Ms. Taylor's blood sugar was extremely low."

"Low?" *She lied about the damn Covid test.* He gritted his teeth as he shook his head slowly. His heart banged harder than a Crip gang in California. Fear coupled with disappointment. he grimaced as he slid down the wall.

"Look, I think she'll be fine." She placed a hand on his shoulders.

He grabbed her hand and peered up into her eyes through his teary ones. "She old, but she strong. At least let me stay the night so I can be here when she wakes up."

"I don't have that pull. I'm sorry. If I did, I wouldn't give a damn how long you stay."

"Okay, I'll leave at four." He surrendered.

The nurse left and the tears fell silently down his face. He pushed himself off the floor and stood beside her bed. He leaned down and kissed her forehead.

"You got to wake up. We all we got, ma." His lips quivered with every word he spoke. He searched her motionless face, but nothing had changed.

"Please? I brought you your favorite. I even got you an order of gizzards on the side," he said, referring to the two piece chicken and biscuit from Williams Chicken. He half smiled as the tears ceaselessly fell.

Bobby used the bottom of his shirt to dry his face and sat on the loveseat next to her. Silently, he prayed, never tearing his eyes from his grandmother.

A few minutes after four, a different nurse strolled in. "Sir, visitation is over."

He stared at the Caucasian nurse menacingly. He wanted to tell her a thing or two, but was afraid his grandmother might hear him. He threw his hoodie on his head and bounced. As he left, he peered back at her room, often, in pursuit of the exit.

I got to stay just a little while longer in case she awakes, he told himself. He peered behind him for the nurse, before entering the restroom. The restroom was bland, but extremely clean.

Fuck it. He opened the last stall and sat down. He would stay until 8pm and then sneak off to her room to see if she had awakened.

"Damn," he blurted, shifting around on the toilet, trying to get comfortable. He locked the stall door, then stared at it unblinkingly as sorrow consumed him, again. Bobby cried silently until he fell into a deep slumber.

Click.

Bobby's eyes shot open at the sound of the stall next to him being opened.

Click.

Click.

Then a whistle.

"Hey. Someone in here?"

Bobby palmed the stall door, and then flushed the toilet. "Yeah." He unlocked the stall and walked out. Instantly, he and the janitor locked eyes.

"Brother, I'm- Did y- you fall asleep or something?"

"Why you say that?" Bobby asked unfazed.

"Well visitation was over at four and the ER is all the way on the other side of the hospital. It's a restroom over there."

Bobby's eyes roamed the older man. He pulled out his iPhone and checked the time. *Shit, I was asleep this long?* It was two minutes past ten.

"Look, I just need you to pretend you didn't see me." Bobby handed him a hundred dollar bill and eased out of the restroom.

The hallway was empty. However, the distance from the restroom to his grandmother's room was pretty lengthy.

I got to be quick. He hurried down the hall and slid into his grandmother's room. He rushed to her side, scanning for any slight movement.

Bobby sighed deeply, then lowered his forehead onto hers. His warm tears feel onto her face and would eventually stain her cheeks. He leaned up.

"I'll see you tomorrow, ma," he whispered before leaving. Bobby slid out of the hospital unnoticed. The Polo G lyrics filled his car as he thought about his grandma the rest of the way home.

Bobby entered his three bedroom home, instantly spotting Jewel on the couch asleep. He did a quick walk through, something he did every time he returned home. He returned and sat on the sofa across form her.

"Jewel," Bobby called out, and shook her lightly. "Jewel."

"Huh?" She slightly opened her eyes. Seeing his face, they widened in fear. She jolted backwards.

"Calm down, girl," Bobby said, eyeing her curiously.

"Whew! I'm sorry, Bobby." She gripped her chest. "I- I just had a bad dream, that's all." She sat up straight, and sat Indian style on the couch.

"You were gone for forever," she yawned.

"Yeah, I know," Bobby responded dryly.

Jewel knew something was wrong, but she was afraid to pry.

"Have you eaten anything?" He asked, unzipping his hoodie.

"Some chips."

"You hungry?"

Her piercing brown eyes locked on his. "You gon' cook?" she smiled.

"Nah, I was just gon' order something." He looked down at his hands. The possibility of his grandmother leaving him forever resurfaced, instantly killing his mood. Bobby stood to his feet.

"On another note, I'm good. Here." He handed her his CashApp card. "Just get you something."

Jewel jumped to her feet. Her eyes searching his. "Bobby, what's wrong? Talk to me. I can see it. I never saw you s-so. I never saw you like this."

Bobby pinched the bridge of his nose. He wanted to just tell her everything from the beginning to the end, but he had only shared that side of him with his grandma. Others didn't even know it existed.

He lifted his head. "Jewel, I'm good. Get you some sleep, and not on the couch. It's two bedrooms you can sleep in. Pick one."

Bobby left Jewel standing there. She sat the card on his table. Somehow, she had lost her appetite, too. She neatly stacked her study books against the wall in the corner and made her way to one of the guest rooms.

Jewel spotted the room to her left. The door was wide open, and she found the room, not just inviting, but impressive.

He has taste.

A sniffing sound halted her steps and diverted her attention. Further down the hallway, light seeped out of the ajar door. Slowly and quietly she walked to it. Nervousness prickled through her. The sniffles grew louder. They were coming from Bobby.

She squinted through the crack in the door. He sat on his bed with his back to her. A physique she could never forget. He stood. The shoulders, the back, and his ass. His uniquely perfect physique drenched the seat of her panties instantly. She rushed back, staring at the ceiling. It was dire that she discovered the source of his pain. She had never seen Bobby so, vulnerable. Something serious had taken place.

But what?

Chapter 25
Blotchy

After picking Jewel up from school, they made a pit stop.

"This is Shandrea."

Jewel gave Shandrea a quick once over, unsure if she wanted to speak. Her beauty was enough to take your breath away, which instantly activated alarms in her mind, making her think that they were possibly more than business partners.

Shandrea knew Jewel was checking her appearance.

"Shandrea, this is Jewel." She smiled, visibly impressed.

"Hey, Jewel. Girl, look, I usually don't do this, but I love my little cousin, so I got you." She paused. "It's simple. A lot of bitches just make the shit hard."

"Okay," Jewel responded, there was no mistaking the timidity. It took Shandrea a little over an hour to cram Jewel with as much information as possible.

"I would've never guessed CPN's were illegal, as freely as people talk about them."

Shandrea chuckled. "Unfortunately, they is, but we have nothing to worry about. The person using it will have to deal with that issue, if it arises."

Shandrea taught Jewel more scams than just the CPN. She could create any document desired, as well as all forms of identification, hard copy and paperback. She knew how to apply and successfully attain a PPP loan, credit card, insurance frauds, and more.

"I know you feel a little overwhelmed. I'm going to have you working with me here at my office until you get the gist of things."

Shandrea's pretty white smile complimented her rich dark skin. Her attractiveness forced Jewel to ponder on her looks without makeup. The glass door flew open. Everyone's heads swiveled in the direction of the door.

"So really, Blotchy?" She paused. Her mug was mean, and her posture and bark were intimidating. "This is the reason you haven't been answering your phone, nigga?"

Blotchy was lost for words. Indya had appeared out of the blue. *Was this bitch following me?* He wondered. He looked back at Jewel and Shandrea, dumbfounded.

Jewel appeared nervous. Shandrea's head was lowered into her phone.

"Nah, nigga, ya location ain't on. This messy bitch told me!" She pointed at Shandrea.

Shandrea gasped sharply. The last thing she expected was for Indya to expose her hand.

"Aww, bitch, cut the act. We ain't cool. I had to pay your greedy ass." She paused. "Fuck you! I didn't come here for you."

Blotchy glared at his cousin, shaking his head. "Tuh, you dead wrong, B."

"Blotchy! I'm talking to you. Answer me!" Veins protruded from Indya's neck as she stood a few feet away with her hands balled into fists. Her banana colored skin turned beat red.

"What?" Blotchy stood to his feet. "What the fuck you want, bruh?" He threw his hands up in the air.

Tears slowly fell from Indya's eyes as she processed everything that was happening. "Really, nigga?" She stepped closer, her eyes resembling slits. "You burn me, bitch ass nigga, and now you clown me in front of the next ho?" She rushed Blotchy, swinging wildly.

Blotchy didn't realize until he felt the sharp sting. "Aaargh." Blotchy placed his hand over his rib cage, while using his other hand to fight her off.

Jewel and Shandrea screamed simultaneously at the sight of blood on his hand.

"Uh-un, I'm calling the police!" Shandrea hollered, reaching for her phone.

Whatever trance Indya was in, she instantly came out of it. Jewel stood against the wall awe-struck and terror stricken. Indya pocketed the knife and dashed out the door.

"She just stood there." Shandrea paused, eyeing Jewel distastefully. "She didn't even pinch the bitch," she continued.

Blotchy turned around and glared at Jewel.

"What? I can't get into any trouble. That'll ruin my plans for college."

"Fuck college. I know people with degrees that's still broke."

Jewel sighed deeply. "Did you give that girl something, Blotchy?" Jewel knew the truth, she just figured it was the perfect opportunity to expose the fact that he did the same to her.

"Why? That's your home girl or somethin'." He eyed her daringly.

"No, I-"

"Yeah, I burnt the bitch, the same day I burnt you. Fuck that ho! I did it to you, just to see where you was mentally. And just like I said before, you's a kid!"

Jewel gasped sharply at his shocking confession. "A kid? How the fuck is that so?"

He minced, easing closer. "A grown ho wouldn't have kept silent and continue to let me fuck. She would've got my script and hers and made sho' we handle that shit together."

Jewel's nostrils flared, as she eyed him in disbelief. "Bitch, so that makes me a kid?" She paused. "I wasn't a kid when we was fucking."

Blotchy wrapped his hand around her throat and shoved her against the wall. A painting rattled before falling just a few inches away from them.

"Oh, I'ma bitch. I got your bitch." He yanked her into his chest by her throat, then forcefully rammed her into the wall, repeatedly, until she lost consciousness. He released his grip and stood back. She hit the ground hard, like a sack of potatoes.

"Don't do that. Uh-uh. No! Blotchy!" Shandrea's screams fell on deaf ears.

Blotchy swung his leg back, and then rammed the toe of his designer shoes into Jewel's face. Her nose erupted like a volcano, splattered blood decorating Shandrea's office. He did it again, and then once in her stomach. He locked eyes with Shandrea before making his exit.

Chapter 26
Myesha

"Stop crying," Big Dooski whispered, wiping the tears away as they fell. He replaced his fingers with his lips as he began to kiss them.

"Do you look at me different now?"

Big Dooski scowled. "Nawl, that will never happen, but I can ensure it won't happen again," he promised.

Myesha squeezed his neck tighter as Big Dooski held her in his arms, as if she was a child. His lips were full and firm against hers. He continued to peck her lips slowly, while easing down her jeans.

Myesha didn't stop him. She didn't want to make him wait another second.

Why wait for something that's going to happen eventually? She asked herself, using her feet to slide the jeans from around her ankles. Myesha leaned up and straddled his lap. Her plump, pretty, pink pussy rested against his t-shirt. He stuck his two fingers into her moistness caressing her button.

"Mmhmm." She leaned back.

"You like that?" He asked, slowly rubbing her clit with his index finger.

"Yes, don't stop." The feeling was indescribable, but it felt better than anything her mother's perverted boyfriend did to her.

"Wrap your legs around me."

She did so, and he stood to his feet, pushing down his joggers to slightly below his knees. His wood stood at attention. He flopped down on the sofa, and helped Myesha out of her shirt, then bra.

He sucked her breasts and stroked his dick at the same time. Her soft, sexy moans turned him on even more. He lifted her up by her ass cheeks and carefully placed her on top of his six-inch penis. Myesha gasped at the sight of it. It may have been short, but it was nearly as thick as a Snapple can.

"I ain't gon' hurt you, shawty. Relax." He licked his lips, while carefully guiding her onto his stiffness.

She hissed like a snake the further he went inside. He short stroked her an inch at a time, until he was entirely inside. Her little pussy fit him like a glove.

"Oooh, shit," be blurted out.

Dooski took his time with Myesha. It was a bit painful for her, but pleasure quickly subdued it. Although, she lacked experience, Myesha's pussy was tight, wet, and odor free. He was more than elated to teach her a thing or two.

Myesha came three times, and he came twice, ending their steamy sex session. Myesha's head rested on his chest as they lay in bed.

"I love you, Dooski." She smiled, peering into his piercing eyes.

"I love you, too." He paused. "Where that nigga stay at?"

She leaned up. "I don't know. He's over my house most of the time."

"This is your house," he responded seriously.

"Right," she hastily agreed. "Dooski?"

"Huh?"

"Please don't do anything that'll get you taken from me."

He smacked his lips. "His fate is sealed, baby girl." He paused. "I'm gon' make sure he keeps his hand and dick to himself."

She wrapped her arms around him. "Bae, you all I got. My sisters living their lives. My momma don't give a fuck about me. Just chill, please?"

He tore his eyes from her tearful ones. He knew there was a possibility things wouldn't go as planned and he could end up in prison with a hefty sentence. "I'd be less than a man if I just let dude get off scot free."

"What do you think I am?" she paused. "I'm the one he did this to."

Big Dooski thought long and hard about how he could get revenge, without threatening his life as well.

Myesha sat completely up. "I got an idea."

Ah'Million

Chapter 27
Bobby

"It's been thirty hours and she still isn't awake." Bobby's fear intensified as the clock continue to tick.

"Thirty hours is nothing compared to the miracles I've seen." The nurse patted him on the shoulder.

Bobby had been at the hospital since visitation started. After the interview with the GQ journalist, Murder recorded one of his latest songs he had been working on. Although he could hardly focus at the studio, he gave it his best shot, in hopes he made the right changes for the best sound.

"Look, I already got it approved through my supervisor to allow you to stay until my shift ends," she paused, "which is in ten minutes."

"Nurse Vaughn, I appreciate you so much. You don't have to talk in circles. I certainly understand, and I'll be departing ASAP."

Nurse Vaughn felt sorry for Bobby. She wanted badly to console him and promise him things would be fine, but she wasn't so sure of it. She'd seen things go as expected, and completely unexpected. Death was far from unordinary, she witnessed it every day. However, she would never tell the guy mourning his grandmother.

"Give me a call, please, when and if she awakes. I'll be here at eleven tomorrow," he spoke through sniffles.

"I sure will. Matter of fact, I'm going to pass the information to the nurse of the next shift, just in case she awakes before I return."

"Thanks," Bobby lowered his head. He walked closer to the railing. He leaned down and kissed his grandmother's forehead.

"Your food has gotten cold, but I'm gon' make sure it's fresh and hot for you tomorrow," he whispered. Bobby looked at his grandmother over his shoulder until he was completely in the hallway.

"Bobby, I got you." Nurse Vaughn patted her pocket on her shirt like Queen Latifah did on *Set It Off.*

Bobby nodded in agreement and proceeded to this truck.

***

Meanwhile, on the other side of town…

"Ouch," Jewel yelped.

"You have to apply a little pressure on it to stop the bleeding." Shandrea quickly jumped into survival mode after Blotchy walked out of her office, leaving Jewel bruised and battered.

"How does it look?" she questioned.

"Well, you have two black eyes and a busted lip."

"My nose feels like it's broken."

"It's possible, but it looks fine." She paused. "The black eyes are hardly noticeable right now, but tomorrow you are going to look like a raccoon."

"I thought Blotchy really cared about me. I can't believe he did this to me." She burst into tears. "I don't know which hurts the worse, the pain from the beating, or knowing he despises me so much as to maliciously do something to this degree."

Shandrea used the wet towel to dab away the dry blood and ceaseless tears. Even after being thrashed, there was no denying Jewel's beauty. Her tears had washed away her eyeliner, falsies, and the light coat of foundation. However, her natural beauty shined bright like diamonds. Moans and grunts filled the room the lower Shandrea squatted to maintain eye level.

"Okay, boo, that's all I can do." She paused. "Now I can add a little foundation around your eyes."

"I'm cool. It's going to be a waste of time 'cause I'm not done crying," Jewel honestly admitted. "I'm ready to go now. My people are probably worried sick about me."

"Okay, come on," Shandrea stood to her feet. She grabbed a hold of Jewels hand, helping her to her feet.

"Shit! It feels like I got hit by a truck!" She winced in pain.

Shandrea felt sorry for the girl. "Come on, drape your arm across my shoulder."

Jewel did so, making it easier for Shandrea to help her to the car.

"Hold on." Shandrea ran back inside, then decided to join in.

Jewel instructed her the route to Bobby's. "Can I ask you something, Shandrea?"

"Go ahead."

Jewel lowered her head. "Why did you tell ol' girl I was here with Blotchy?" She asked, peering in Shandrea's direction, but Shandrea's eyes were focused on the road ahead, so she thought.

"I don't know. That was foolish of me. But if you forgive me today, you'll never have to question my loyalty tomorrow."

That statement alone was enough for Jewel. She hadn't known Shandrea for twenty-four hours, but there was something about her tone that ceased any uncertainty.

Jewel was silent whenever she wasn't instructing. She didn't know if she wanted to be completely honest with Bobby, or tell him a lie.

"Okay, we're here," Shandrea spoke softly. Guilt coupled with sorrow consumed her. She felt responsible for Jewel being attacked.

"You don't have to wait, I'm good." Jewel unbuckled her seatbelt.

"Here, at least take my number."

Jewel listened attentively while programming Shandrea's number into her phone. She wanted to say more, but all she could muster was a sincere apology.

Jewel slid out of Shandrea's black Charger and walked up the driveway. Her heart was heavier than someone who had just suffered a great loss.

"What you, Jewel?" Bobby's brows drooped in confusion. "What happened?" He grabbed her face, swiftly scanning the damage.

"I got jumped," she lied.

Bobby pushed the door open and led her inside

"Who jumped you?"

Jewel eased onto the sofa.

Bobby looked at her with obvious concern. Her beauty was moving, enough to distract him from the task at hand.

"Bobby, can I, can I just stay here a few days? I don't want to be at home by myself."

Bobby sighed deeply as he thought long and hard. If Kad got a whiff of his precious little girl staying with a grown ass man, he'd surely flip out.

"Yeah." He paused, lowered his head. "Keep that between the two of us."

"Okay."

"Now, tell me everything."

Jewel sighed deeply before mentally assembling a story together that Bobby would find believable. He listened attentively as she began to ramble off. Bobby was in no position to console anyone, but Jewel needed him. If she didn't, she would have gone home.

"Shower or bath?" Bobby asked, standing to his feet.

"I'd like to bathe. I don't think I can stand for too long." She winced.

"Come on." Bobby helped her off the couch and placed his hand in the middle of her back, carefully following her as she slowly led the way.

Jewel slid into the room and Bobby headed for the restroom. He adjusted the temp on the water to assure it was just right for Jewel, as he waited for it to fill up.

"Jew-shit!" He tore his eyes from her.

"I'm sorry, I thought you would at least wait until you got to the bathroom to undress," he yelled from the hallway.

"I been doing it this way since I was a kid." She paused. "I'm sorry."

Bobby shook the image from his head and headed to the kitchen. If only a snap of the finger could erase the image, he'd be fine. But it left a permanent mess that only time could remove. Her box was slick and bald like Michael Jordan's head, and her skin was blemish free.

Bobby heard the door to the bathroom shut, and he moved around the kitchen with a purpose. He didn't have much of an appetite, but he wanted to certainly take care of hers. During his prison stint was when Bobby discovered his passion for cooking. The delicious aroma forced Jewel to put a little pep in her step.

Damn, this nigga can cook, too?

Lost in his thoughts, Bobby never heard Jewel enter the kitchen, until he turned around and spotted her.

"Is that my shirt?" Bobby asked turning back around to face the stove.

"Of course, silly." She paused. "I forgot to pack my night clothes."

With his back facing her, he nodded his head in agreement.

"What you cook?"

"Shrimp and sausage Alfredo, steamed broccoli, and garlic bread."

"That sounds delicious." Jewel rubbed her tummy.

Out of the corner of his eye, he could see the t-shirt rise and fall, exposing her plump butt cheeks.

"Hold on." Bobby quickly left the kitchen to retrieve a pair pajama pants.

She was cleaning up his mess when he entered. He gritted his teeth to refrain from being aroused, but seeing her ass hanging out from underneath her shirt provoked him twice as much.

"Put these on." Bobby tossed the pajamas at Jewel.

Her smile faded after realizing what he took the time to go and retrieve. She smacked her lips and sat at the dinner table.

Bobby neatly stacked the food on the plates, then carefully placed them on the table, before taking a seat across from Jewel.

"Have more respect for yourself. you too beautiful for that ho' shit."

Even in pain, she heard his compliment loud and clear. She looked at him but turned away from his piercing eyes. Both of their pains ran deeper than an ocean, and the brief time their eyes locked, they perceived it instantly.

Her bruises made it hard for him to tear his eyes from the damage. It was something off with her story. But he would just have to believe it for now, at least until he heard the other side, which he'd probably never hear because it wasn't any of his business.

"Since I told you what was going on with me, do you care to share?" She asked in between bites.

It bothered Bobby to know his pain was so transparent. "Nah, talking about it don't change shit anyways." He stood to his feet. "It's getting late." He glanced at his watch. "Shouldn't you be getting you some rest for school?"

"I'm not going." Jewel picked up the shrimp with her hand, ate it, and then seductively sucked the juice off of her finger.

"Yo pop cool with that, Jew?"

"Bobby, look at my face," she yelled, pushing her plate further away. Tears began to fall.

Bobby lowered his head, unsure of how to respond. Then Jewel took off towards the room. He deeply sighed, then gathered the plates, cleaning up before going to bed. He stopped by Jewel's room before going to his own, but opted against going in. There was only so much he could say, and those words had already been spoken. He flopped down onto his California King sized bed, as he prayed aloud.

"Lord, please give my grandmother the strength to win this battle. Amen."

Bobby removed his shirt, then jeans, and climbed into his bed. He turned his TV on ESPN, and half listened to the commentator. He turned on his side and closed his eyes, but sleep never came.

Time passed as he tossed and turned, flipping and repositioning his pillows, just trying to get a good night's sleep. Finally, Bobby had given up. He swung his legs off the bed and sat calmly on the edge. He glanced at his phone in hopes of seeing a missed call from possibly one of the nurses, but the only person who had called was Kesha.

He stood and headed out of his bedroom to retrieve a drink of water, when he realized he wasn't the only one inside of the house.

He had company. He pulled a pair of basketball shorts over his navy blue briefs, then proceeded to the kitchen. Bobby wasn't trying to be nosey but is sounded like Jewel was crying and talking to someone.

"I just can't believe this," she repeated twice more. She was talking to Myesha. "He didn't have to do me like that" she whined.

He? Bobby knew there was more to it. Luckily, he had just found out. He went to the kitchen and grabbed both of them a bottled water. It was silent when he returned, minus the sniffles. He opened the door.

Jew?" She looked over her shoulder. Seeing that it was Bobby, she quickly dried her face with her bare hands.

"Huh?" She slid up against the head board.

"You good? I heard you crying."

"I'll be ok." She nodded, her lip quivering.

"Here, drink this." He handed her the water. "Talk to me." He sat on the edge of the bed.

Tears filled her almond shaped eyes. Pulling Bobby's heart strings instantly. "I just don't understand. I've lost everyone." She paused. "I don't know when he's coming home." Jewel burst out into a tearful sob.

Bobby felt compelled to swoop her into a tight hug. He wanted to cease her tears and momentarily take the pain away. The familiar masculine fragrance of his favorite cologne floated into her personal space, reminding her of her dad, forcing her to wail like a wounded animal.

"Jew, uh-un, don't do that. I got you. It's gon' be alright," Bobby assured, rocking her back and forth.

"Sssshhh," he told her as he used his other hand to rub the top of her head.

"You just don't understand how it feels to lose two of the people you care about the most."

His hand immediately stopped its comforting massage.

"You truly believe that?" Bobby asked her with a solidness she'd never seen before in any being on Earth.

Jewel's eyes widened. "I-I mean, Bobby, I don't know anything about you. You never talk. Can you relate to how I feel?" She demanded to know. Her voice sounded like she was aching, holding back from crying.

Bobby wanted to express his sorrow, merely because it felt like the perfect time. At that moment, he wanted to grieve his father and mother, with hopes that he wouldn't have to grieve his grandmother.

"Talk to me." Jewel begged in a whisper-like tone. "Bobby?"

His tangy male scent filled her as their mouths merged. His lips were full and firm against hers. Sparks flashed as their tongues danced. His strong masculine aura surrounded her. Exciting her.

She flipped the sheet to the side that once covered her hidden assets. A lime green bra and boy shorts covered her goodies, and Bobby took his time peeling the both of them off.

He stood to his feet and removed his briefs and shorts in one swift motion. His eight-inch pole was thick and long, coated in caramel, drenching the inside of her mouth instantly. He leaned down and kissed Jewel's soft lips with a wet slow peck.

"Fuck that nigga that you think you found."

He pushed her on her back and climbed into the bed. He planted a trail of kisses from her forehead to her feet. Heat pulsed through her. He positioned himself in between her legs, and rubbed his dick against her love button and down to her opening repeatedly, until she began to beg.

"Ple-please, fuck me, Bobby." She moaned soft and seductively, as their eyes locked.

Bobby dug himself inside of her and she squirmed uncontrollably.

"It hurts, Bobby." She palmed his chest.

Bobby grabbed both of her hands, then held them in place above her head with his left hand. He eased himself in, her wetness inviting his length. Completely in, he plunged himself in and out of her wetness. The feeling was so pleasant Bobby's toes happen to entangle.

"Didn't I tell you I got you?"

He rotated and thrust his pole into her warm box. Feeling himself on the verge of an eruption, he slid his hands underneath Jewel's body. He gripped her shoulders and flipped her over.

Bobby lay on his back with Jewels nude, sticky body covering his. She rested her forehead on top of his. The two of them using it as an opportunity to catch their breath. Jewel pressed her plump lips onto Bobby's. A kiss exchanged between the two so passionate that only an image could describe it. It was too profound for words.

He firmly gripped her shoulders, pulling her body down onto his eight inches, while he thrust upward, touching places that she had no clue existed. Moans and grunts filled the room.

Never in a million years did she think this would happen. Many nights, she dreamed, and many days, she fantasized about having sex with Bobby. A touch, a kiss, or even a hug would suffice, but the pleasure he was blessing her with now, was even better.

Bobby drilled away all the sorrow and pent-up pressure. However, he took Jewel's hurt into consideration as well. His strokes were slow, deep, meticulous, and purposeful. He sexed her with the intent to heal wounds, fill voids, and mend her heart that had been broken. Bobby never recalled a time in his life he fucked a female like he was fucking Jewel, neither did he have the desire to.

He wanted to give her love and loyalty. He just hoped he could do it, instead of just thinking it, and refrain from allowing the person he had become to ruin his shot at an opportunity for love, which he secretly yearned for.

Jewel came so hard her thighs trembled. Shortly after, Bobby exploded inside of the pretty young thang.

***

Kad was adamant about putting out one of Blotchy's albums before giving him his own imprint, so that meant mad studio time. Bobby figured he'd start early. He planned on making it to see his grandmother on time. Bobby left Jewel some cash on the counter and proceeded to his destination.

Kad had signed a form to release all his property to Bobby, giving him access to his home. Bobby arrived ten minutes early and straightened up anything out of order. Seeing the picture of Jewel and her mother saddened him. Trials and tribulations had forced her into situations that tainted her innocence.

A knock startled him. He peered out of the blinds, then opened the door for Blotchy. Bobby forced himself to put his perspective of Blotchy to the back of his mind and focus on getting the album done, so they all could get paid. He was full of arrogance and pride. Bobby could smell it on him.

"Whad up? You good?" He asked, stepping inside. Bobby stepped to the side, allowing him to enter.

A few scratches exposed his pink meat on the side of both his eyes. "Damn, you good?"

Blotchy frowned. "Yeah, I had a fight with my bitch."

"Keep straight, it's the last door on the left."

Blotchy slowly proceeded, as if he was some sort of tourist in a foreign country. He discreetly peaked inside of the rooms.

Suddenly, it dawned on Bobby. "You looking for ol' girl who showed you the way to the studio last time, huh?"

Blotchy stopped and turned around. "Nah, it's just nice in here, that's all," he lied.

Shit, if I was you, I'd be checking for her, too. "Good 'cause she off limits," Bobby said, pushing the door to the studio open.

"Tuh." Blotchy smirked.

Chapter 28
Kad

"You know I got you. Those chicks going to get what's coming to them for lying." Sierra spoke into the receiver, her eyes fixated on Kad's.

He wasn't stressing like he had been the first couple of days. Knowing that he had his man's, Bobby, and a ride or die chick, willing to break the bank in exchange for his freedom, he simply let go and let time. Sierra had showed up in a time of need, proving herself. He didn't want to fill her head with jail talk. However, inwardly, he knew just how much his feelings deepened for her since his incarceration.

"I really appreciate you, for real. Shit, will you testify on my behalf?" Kad placed the chips on the counter.

"I got you, zaddy, anything you need."

"Times up," The CO announced. He was some big, burly dude with orange hair.

Kad stood to his feet, so did Sierra.

"Don't forget to let Bobby know I'm slidin' through to pick up the keys to the office."

"Bet."

She watched Kad until he disappeared around the corner. She had some important phone calls she needed to make.

***

At the hospital…

"I would've called sooner, but I wanted to be sure that she wouldn't slip off into another one" the nurse informed. She had contacted Bobby thirty minutes before eleven, cutting his studio time short. He wasted no time getting to the hospital.

"You good." He moved past her and into the room. Bobby and his grandmother instantly locked eyes.

She flashed her pearly white teeth, warming his heart. Overjoyed, he rushed to his grandma and wrapped his arms around her the best way he could, in spite of the railing being in the way.

"Aww, ma, why you lie to me?" He searched her eyes.

Although she looked a bit drained, she had air in her lungs and she was alive. She deeply sighed.

"I'm sorry, baby. I didn't want you to worry." She peered around, then paused. "Truth is, I been eating that there chicken I like for seven days a week." She cut her eyes toward the box of chicken.

"How? I-"

"Door dash." She lowered her head.

Bobby shook his head. "You know better, ma."

"I know, I know. It's just so good to me." She smiled, then reached up and squeezed his hand.

"Ma." He clasped both hands around hers.

"Huh?"

"Promise me you gon' take better care of yourself. If anything close to this happens again, you moving in with me."

She sighed deeply. "Alright."

Chapter 29
Myesha

Bey peered back at Myesha with a glare imparting so much hatred that it sent chills down her spine.

"The defendant's bond is set at 250,000 dollars." The judge banged the gavel, then stood to leave.

"I got something for you, bitch," Bey mouthed discreetly to Myesha.

She knew just how grimy her mother could be and she wanted no dealings with her whatsoever. Panic seeped in as Myesha snaked her head around swiftly. It felt as if the four walls were closing in as Myesha's heart began to race abnormally. She placed her purse into Big Dooski's lap and flew out of the courtroom. She clutched the lower part of her stomach and covered her mouth in fear she'd vomit. She darted inside the restroom, and into the nearest empty stall, where she released all of the contents she had consumed earlier that morning. Once she was sure she was done, she used the tissue to wipe her mouth, then the toilet.

Myesha flopped down onto the toilet seat, drained and fully clothed. She took deep breaths, as she prepared to re-enter the courtroom. The door to the restroom opened. Myesha reached around to flush the toilet.

"Ssshhh."

Hearing that, she opted against it. The sound of Kad's name caused her to stiffen. The voices were unfamiliar, increasing the desire to see the faces of the women. Myesha turned on the voice recorder on her phone and began recording the conversation. No one would believe her if she repeated the things that spewed from their mouths.

"I'm doing you a favor. Don't act sweet now because things are getting serious. This can sabotage my marriage if things go left!" said one girl.

"If it goes right, you won't need your husband anymore. If you keep doubting me, you're going to end up with his lil' dick ass forever," the second girl responded.

Myesha heard one of them sigh deeply. Then the girl said to the other, "Come on."

I have to tell Jewel, Myesha thought.

Chapter 30
Myesha

Tooh! The thick goo hung from the tip of her mink lashes, like ornaments on a Christmas tree. Myesha Scowled. The foul scent only angered her even more.

Since when does spit have a smell on it? Funky breath bitch.

She blinked rapidly as her mother swung at her wildly, yelling obscenities. Dooski snatched her up immediately, restricting her movements. She'd seen her mother angry before, but never had she witnessed a wrath like this one. She cringed, despising the way her mother acted in a place as public as the courts.

"You wrong!"

"He didn't do anything you didn't want him to do! You trash, just like your sisters!"

With her mother refusing to stop, Myesha covered her ears to drown out her voice. She ran past her mother and the rest of the people, who stood around watching the show.

I hope Dooski don't believe those lies.

Tears filled her eyes. Her mother had sabotaged everything else. She hoped Bey didn't convince him to disown her, too.

Honk!

She gasped sharply at the realization of a near miss. Shaking like a stripper, Myesha stopped, afraid to move. Perhaps this time she'd get struck.

"Bitch, get out the way!"

Move.

She couldn't, in the midst of mentally battling with herself. A set of hands gently shoved her in the back. The shove may have lacked aggression, yet it possessed enough urgency to snap Myesha out of her trance.

"Get out the car and make us get out the way, fuck boy!"

It was Dooski, at her rescue again. His devotion only stirred more emotions, forcing the tears to fall freely. How could he care so much? He could've disowned her after they had sex. That was what most guys his age did anyway. He took Myesha by the hand and led her to the car.

"You good?" Deep concern was embedded in his expression, as he looked her up and down. "I got you, mama." It was something he had started calling her since the day they made their relationship official.

She believed him. Who else did she have to believe in? Surely not in herself. Growing up, Bey said nothing but harsh things to her and her sisters, and she had become accustomed to it, so she thought. Oddly, today her words stung like alcohol poured on a fresh wound. The next morning, Myesha had every intent on attending school, especially since finding out about the women plotting against her uncle. She hit the snooze button on her alarm clock, without even opening her eyes to see the time.

There's always tomorrow.

Knock! Knock! Knock!

Panicky and confused, Myesha's eyes fluttered open. Afraid it was the police, or maybe her mother, she nudged Dooski, who was still asleep bedside her.

There was the knock again.

"Who the hell is that?" Dooski questioned aloud. Climbing out of bed simultaneously, they dragged to the door, Dooski leading the way. Without looking in the peephole, he snatched the door open. Confusion etched his face.

"Brandi?" Myesha asked.

She was the last person Myesha expected.

"Can I come in?"

She looked from Myesha to Dooski. She batted her long lashes, gracefully exposing her pearly whites.

"It's cool, bae. This is my sister."

Dooski hadn't met neither of her sisters, and the look on his face simply told he didn't care to meet them.

"Brandi, what are you doing here?"

Dooski was already in pursuit to the bedroom as Brandi stepped inside. There was a pause after she asked the question, but it only last until Dooski was out of ear shot.

"What did she do to you?" Brandi asked.

"What do you mean?" Myesha replied.

Brandi flopped down on the couch. "I mean what I'm saying."

"He molested me," Myesha admitted, her eyes trained to the floor.

Brandi silently nodded as she processed the information.

"Um, she's still on that bullshit," she said, crossing her legs. "It's everyone's fault but hers," she continued, as Dooski emerged from the room. He veered into the kitchen, but exited as quickly as he entered.

"Bae, I'll be back. You want something while I'm out?" He leaned down and hugged her small frame tightly.

"I'm ok." She smiled weakly. He planted a kiss on her forehead and left. Myesha placed her phone face down on the sofa and cleared her throat.

"He good to you?" Brandi raised her left brow.

"Yeah, I like him." Myesha wasted no time responding. In her eyes, he was proven. Proven to be more loyal than kin.

"Well that's all that matters." Brandi's lingering stare caused Myesha instant discomfort. Their once strong bond had weakened, due to distance.

"What?" Myesha asked, after swallowing the lump in her throat.

"Sissy." She paused. "It's cool he's good to you, but sometimes you need to make sure you're OVER GOOD to yourself."

Ah'Million

Chapter 31
Blotchy

A few days had passed since Blotchy and Jewel spoke. "Aye fam, where did you drop my bitch off at?" This was the seventh time he dialed Shandrea, and the first time she answered.

"Damn, I see where you called. I was busy with a client." She paused. Loud smacking and slurping noises filled the phone.

"Damn, is you still busy with the *client*?" He put emphasis on the word client. His words were laced with sarcasm.

Shandrea burst out laughing. "Nah, nigga, I'm feeding my face." She paused. "But about your girl, I didn't take her to a certain location. I did enter a residential area, and she told me she'll walk the rest of the way."

"Damn," he mumbled. "Alright bet. I'll talk to you later," he continued, disconnecting the call before she could respond. He figured Jewel would be smarter. Shandrea wouldn't get a second opportunity to put her in a cross.

"Dooski," he shouted, entering the smoke shop.

"Sup, Gangsta?" Dooski shot back, emerging from the rear.

"Where my bitch at, Dooski?"

Appalled, Dooski jolted backwards. "Yo bitch?" He paused. "The hell if I know." He threw his hands up.

"You might not know, but ya girl do." Blotchy smirked.

"Probably so, but she hasn't been to my crib."

"Have Myesha invite her over."

"Then what?" Dooski challenged.

"I'm gon' pop out on her ass. What you mean?"

Blotchy's stance was threatening. However, confusion, instead of fear, etched Dooski's face. He stood back and looked Blotchy from his head to feet.

"Bruh, you tripping." Dooski turned to walk away.

Blotchy reached out and grabbed his shoulder.

Dooski jerked away from his grasp.

"So, you ridin' with them ho's?" Blotchy accused.

"Nawl, but I don't want no drama at my doorstep, where me and my bitch lay our heads," Dooski admitted seriously.

Obnoxious laughter escaped from Blotchy lips. "Ol sucka ass, you haven't been with this bitch three months."

"If I'm a sucka, what that make you, Busta?" He paused. "Me and Myesha hooked up the same day you and Jewel did. Look at you, ready catch a charge behind this bitch. The fuck on!"

Blotchy turned his mouth downward and nodded silently, as he watched his friend for years storm out of the store.

He gritted his teeth as he watched him until he was no longer in sight. Blotchy and Dooski had been boys for forever. Being able to relate on so many levels had strengthened their bond. Dooski had lost his brother a few years ago. Although Blotchy lost his younger brother a decade ago, the two men had experienced and shared the same pain, allowing them both to try and fill that emptiness from the loss of someone they held so close to their heart.

Chapter 32
Bobby

"Watch ya step," Bobby coached. He held his grandmother's hands tightly as he peered into her eyes while backpedaling through the foyer of her home. She was concentrating so hard that she remained silent until she was safely seated on the sofa, afraid to open her mouth in fear of being thrown off balance.

Bobby was as ecstatic as a kid on Christmas day. Nothing and no one left on God's green earth could compete, nor compare, with the love that he had for his grandmother. After losing his mother and father years ago, his grandmother was all that he had left.

"Whew." She tilted her head towards the ceiling. She looked up at him and smiled faintly, exhausted, yet evidently relieved.

He smiled back genuinely at his grandmother, not simply returning the gesture. Truthfully, he had so many reasons to smile, thankful that she was still kicking at such a ripe age. A lot of big mamas had passed on, especially the ones that were birthed in the times of depression and slavery, the ones that invited the whole hood inside for a plate and a place to stay, if need be. They even had a remedy for every illness in general. Big mommas nowadays fought and clubbed with you, instead of praying and attending church with you. Luckily, Bobby still had his big momma. He walked behind the sofa, where she sat, and gently stroked her salt and pepper hair. It was long and thin. The cocoa butter scent brushed his nostrils immediately, taking him to a place a while ago.

He had walked in on his grandmother squirting the lotion in her hand and massaging it through her tresses. He asked, "Ma, why you put lotion in your hair?"

"It keeps your hair soft and hydrated." This was another one of her famous remedies. She knew anytime Bobby inquired about something, then lingered around, he wanted it. She squirted a nice amount onto her hand and palmed his fade repeatedly.

"Thanks, granny," he darted into the direction he had come from.

Bobby smiled, flashing back on that day. Hovering behind but over his grandmother, Bobby could tell she had fallen asleep by the way her chest heaved up and down. He walked around and planted a kiss on her forehead. The house was still the same way he had left it, clean. knowing his grandmother would feel the total opposite, he removed his Amiri shirt and black AP and went to work. Minutes later, the loud knock at the door startled Bobby. He froze. The only thing that moved was his brows as they dipped in confusion.

Who in the hell?

He proceeded down the long hallway. A menacing mug plastered across his face the closer he got to the door. He cut his eyes at his grandmother. She was oblivious to the knock on the door. She had fallen into a deep sleep. She had begun to snore. He dipped and peered through the small slit on the blinds, without touching them. A short, bald, white guy stood on the other side of the door. He held a clipboard in one hand, and a small brown box in the other. His clothes were a little too snug for Bobby's liking, but he went ahead and opened the door anyway.

"Sir, I have a delivery for an R. Taylor."

Faggot ass nigga.

The sassiness in his voice ran Bobby hot. You would've thought the guy winked at him or something. He opened the door a little wider, so delivery boy could see his grandmother.

"She right there, asleep. I'll sign for her."

He appeared slightly hesitant but handed Bobby the pen and clipboard anyway. With his eyes trained on the package, Bobby accepted both the box and receipt. Then he shut the door. He usually wouldn't pry, but since finding out she lied about her eating habits, it was a different story.

It's probably some damn chicken.

He chuckled, tearing open the box. The thin gold necklace shined like a fresh coat of gloss. The pendant was unique. Bobby's brow rose in admiration. It was two hands intertwined, forming a fist-like shape. The pendant was no bigger than her thumb nail, yet it spoke huge volumes. There was no sender's name on the box, but inside was a small note.

*Two is better than one, and I trust you with
my life. I love you dear sister in Christ.*
Sincerely, Sister K

He placed the note back inside the box. He assumed the gift was from a friend of hers at the church. His grandmother had been involved in the church since he could remember. He was forced to board the church van every Wednesday and Sunday, and even additional days in the summertime. Wednesdays was choir practice, a band for kids four to fourteen years old, known as the Sunshine band. Bobby smiled reminiscing on those days.

"My name is Bobby and I love the lord."

He chuckled softly, reflecting on the day like it was yesterday. His grandmother's laughter caught him by surprise. She made her way into the kitchen. Despite moving at a snail's pace, Bobby was relieved to see her moving.

"Those were the days." She flashed that angelic smile.

"Is this mine?" She sat down. "You know, opening people mail is a felony offense," she joked, removing the necklace. She gasped sharply, holding the necklace up.

"It's beautiful." Her brows dipped in confusion. "Who-"

Bobby handed her the note out of the box. Immediately, a slow smile spread across her face.

"Put this on for me, baby."

Ring. Ring.

After placing her necklace on her neck, he picked up his phone. It was Jewel.

Ah'Million

Chapter 33
Jewel

Jewel didn't know where Bobby's grandmother stayed but she knew it wasn't around the corner, so she'd decided to follow the crowd. Two of the popular girls at her school decided to finally let their hands talk instead of the back and forth rah-rah. Everyone was crunk, anxious and excited, ready to see who would win out of the two. Jewel didn't give a damn. This was her kind of hype. The meet up place to fight was always behind the smoke shop. She just hoped the distraction would be big enough to keep her presence undetected.

"I'm 'bout to smash this ho," the chubbier one yelled.

They walked on opposite sides of the street, but in the same direction. The slimmer one said nothing. She just kept walking. She didn't seem amped or crunk. However, she didn't look afraid, either. Jewel's heart raced thunderously. She was afraid for the girl. The closer they got, the more Jewel palms dampened. With one hand, she dried them on her denim jeans. With the other, she phoned Myesha.

"Hey, bitch!"

"Hey, girl," Jewel shot back.

"Why you sound all dry? And what's all that noise in the background?" Myesha asked.

"Girl, Princess and Shayla about to fight.

"Bitch what?" She screamed. "Damn, I should've went to school."

"Calm down, and who is that?" Jewel asked, hearing the voice in the background.

"Girl, I'm with Brandi."

"Oh okay." Uncertainty laced Jewel words. Brandi was the last person she was expecting to hear.

"Um. Where y'all going?" Jewel pried.

"Secure a bag."

Money wasn't an issue, but knowing the way Brandi got hers, Jewel wanted no parts of it.

"Hey, I got to go, Jewel. I love you. Let me know who won that fight."

Click.

Jewel sighed deeply as she slowed her stride. She wanted to make sure she blended in with everyone else. She shot Bobby a text to let him know she was by the smoke shop. Once he arrived, she would run to the front of the store.

A circle was already formed around the two girls, once Jewel arrived. She still had a good view of it. She pulled her phone out and recorded it for Myesha. The chubbier one was still crunk.

"Yeeaahh," she screamed, bouncing around like she was a professional boxer.

The slim one wrapped her box braids around in a bun. One of the chubbier girl's friends handed her a scrunchy for her hair. She declined her offer.

"I'm good, this bitch ain't gon' even touch me."

She pulled up her Khaki's. The slim one pulled up hers, too. They posted up, then rushed one another simultaneously. The slim one was quicker. The chubby one just a tad bit slower and sloppier. Both girls landed punches. The slim one's licks were more effective and precise. Afraid of taking another lick, the chubby one dropped her head and went in for a bear hug type move.

Bink. Bink.

Two uppercuts to the chin gave the chubby girl noodle legs, and she fell slowly onto her knees. She hooked her swiftly in the temple, making her fall on her back. The crowd erupted. There were a few boos but Shayla had won the fight.

Loud music blasted.

Bad and she thick, pop that pussy like a clip. She in school but she strip. Use two hands when she eat the dick.

Screams erupted.

Jewel peered through the crowd. One of the older chicks from her school was stripped down to just her boy shorts. She twerked and bounced her ass on Blotchy's lap to the beat.

Jewel gritted her teeth. She clenched her phone with trembling fingers. Jewel could tell he liked it by the way he bit his bottom lip. She began flashing back on the few times they had sex. Jewel bent down to tie her shoelaces.

Fuck this.

The sound of her phone halted her movements.

"Hello," she answered, looking around.

"I'm here, where you at?" Concern laced his words. He must have spotted the crowd.

"Here I come." She hung up. As bad as she wanted to approach him and his chick, she eagerly walked to Bobby's truck. Blotchy may have ruffled her feathers, but nothing fazed her when she was in the presence of the man of her dreams.

"Hey, Bobby," she greeted cheerfully, immediately forgetting the reason she was mad to begin with. She slammed the door shut then reached in and wrapped her arms around his neck. Bobby pushed her hands down.

"Chill with all that, Jewel." Her brows dipped in confusion. They'd just had amazing sex last night. Now this. Jewel discreetly swallowed the lump in her throat.

"Look, Jewel." He paused. Then turned her way. His honey irises made her clit pit-a-pat. She looked away. There was no point in steady lusting after something she couldn't have. He grabbed her by the chin gently, turning her head in his direction.

"Look, what happened last night is not happening again. It was a mistake. A mistake you need to keep between us."

"I didn't tell no one," she spoke between clenched teeth.

"Cool."

She turned and peered out of the window. But the only thing she could see was a blur from the tears that clouded her vision. She thought they had something special, and he thought it was a mistake. Jewel had possessed a strong infatuation for Bobby since an adolescent. She had finally gotten what she prayed for, and it meant everything to her. Yet, to him, it meant nothing, nothing at all.

Ah'Million

Chapter 34
Myesha

"Hey, cousin," Myesha greeted, opening the door for Jewel. She had caught an Uber to Myesha's crib, which she shared with Dooski, since she couldn't stop her mind from wondering.

"Hey, girl." Jewel wasn't as cheerful.

"What was Brandi doing over here?"

Myesha's appearance forced the inquiry to come forth. Her long bundles flowed beneath her ass cheeks. She glowed like she had been kissed by the sun. But there was something else that was different, which Jewel couldn't pin-point at the moment.

"Come on, let's take a ride," Myesha suggested, snatching the alarm pad off the table.

"Bae," she called out.

"Yeah," Dooski answered.

"I'll be back. I'm about to run Jewel to the store."

Dooski emerged from the back.

"What's up, Jewel." He paused, sizing her up. "You good?"

"I'm okay, missing my cousin, that's all."

He nodded but his eyes never left hers. Addressing the elephant in the room, Myesha stood on the tips of her toes and wrapped her arms around his neck.

"See you later, bye." She grabbed Jewel by the forearm, dragging her out of the apartment.

"What's up with him?" Jewel asked, once they were outside.

"I don't know, and I don't give a shit." Myesha hit the alarm.

"I can't believe he letting you drive his car and yo' ass don't even have a license."

She shrugged and smiled mischievously. Once inside, Myesha tossed Jewel a kush blunt. Like a strong cup of coffee on an early morning, it was exactly what Jewel needed. It was like applying pressure to her bleeding wound. She put fire to the weed and leaned back in the seat.

And when shit get bad, I get in my bag.

But I thought you'd be the one that I could lean on.
Now I'm in that gym, got my waist on slim.
You can still see that ass with the jeans on.
Now you see me up when you send that text,
And I don't even respond.

They both sang along to the lyrics, as Myesha pulled into the lot of the Exxon. She parked by the entrance of the store, then turned the music down.

"Spill the beans, bitch." Jewel leaned up in her seat, giving Myesha a cheesy grin.

"Well, first of all, I went and got dolled up. Brandi introduced me to her photographer, and I took these." She scrolled through her phone and turned the screen in Jewel's direction.

Jewel gasped in shock as Myesha showed her every photo she had taken yesterday. Her eyes grew two sizes as she looked on in confusion, and admiration. Every photo revealed at least one, if not all, of her assets.

"You look damn good, but why you doing this? Dooski takes damn good care of you."

"Bitch, ever since I started my *Only Fans,* my shit been doing numbers. You have to send me a hundred dollars just to look at this shit. I'm uploading my videos next."

Jewel looked at her cousin in disbelief.

"Jewel, your shit would really pop. You should do it." Myesha tried to convince her.

"I don't want to hear that. I'm going to college." Jewel paused. "What else do you have to tell me?" She continued.

Myesha sighed deeply. "It's your dad."

"What about him?"

"Check this out."

Chapter 35
Kad

Kad sat across from Bey in the visitation room. Bey had grabbed him a few things out of the vending machine before sitting down. His stomach growled continuously, like a vicious dog right before an attack. However, his soda hadn't been opened, and he had hardly eaten any of the chips. Pity engulfed him, like Hurricane Katrina had done the city of New Orleans. It had been years since his older sister indulged in the potent drug. He listened as she rambled on.

The way his eyes searched hers, anyone with eyes could easily see his sincerity. However, her words were his least concern. He examined her thoroughly, forcing himself to accept the unfamiliar person in front of him. Surely it wasn't his kin. Her once full face had slimmed in just a matter of weeks. Her eyes were darker than any night, wintry or hot. The bags under her eyes could carry a cart of groceries. Her breath reeked of vomit, and the discoloration of her teeth indicated that she had been vomiting.

"All I need is some money."

Kad hadn't heard anything come out of her mouth, until now. It was like someone had paused then unpaused their conversation. She was still talking when Kad cut her off.

"Wait, what about the money?" He scowled.

"You all I got, Kad." Tears welled in her eyes before she lowered her head. "And I'm all he's got. The case is bogus, and a good attorney could get him off."

Kad's nostrils flared. "You want me to help you, help a nigga that done touched my niece?"

"That's a lie, Kad! I wouldn't be sitting there defending him, if that was the case."

Kad slightly chuckled.

"You doing the same shit you did with Mark. Look at you. You just don't know how to be alone?"

His menacing scowl and the truth that fell from his lips forced her to drop her head in shame.

"You the reason Bianca and Brandi so fucked up," he yelled.

The tears spilled down her cheeks like a cup that had run over. "I know. I know. I know," she spoke in between sniffles. "What about me? What about my happiness?" She lifted her head, jabbing herself in the chest with her index finger.

Same ol' Bey, still about self.

"Look, I'm going to give you five grand, and not a cent over. I'm not just giving you this because I care about your happiness, but I'm also paying you to stay away from Myesha and Jewel." He stood to his feet. "Sir, I'm done." He turned his back to Bey.

"Thanks, Bro." Bey left as quickly as she had come.

Kad rushed into his dorm to call Bobby.

"What's going on?" Kad asked, as soon as he heard Bobby's voice.

"I just stung for fifty racks. I just picked to meet with a female investor. I'm not as good as you with words but, I never heard the word *NO* dealing with women."

Kad erupted with laughter. "That's what's up. How's my baby?"

"She's good, she at the crib."

"Cool. Look, I need you to shoot Bey five stacks."

"Bet."

"Oh, and Sierra supposed to be contacting you so she can help around the office."

"Bruh," Bobby sighed deeply. "I don't need no help."

"She good, fam. I trust her. Just think about it."

"I don't have to. You trust her. She can come through when you get out."

Kad chuckled slightly. He should have known Bobby would disagree, especially with everything going on. There was no way he was going to place himself in a position to end up like *R. Kelly.*

"Okay, cool. Well look, tell my baby I love her, and I'll give her a call later. I'll call you tomorrow, after my visit with my attorney."

"Alright, boy, I love you."

"Hey, have Blotchy been recording?"

"It's been a few days, but I'm working on it."
"Alright, peace."

Ah'Million

Chapter 36
Jewel

Someone was out there praying on her downfall.

Jewel stood in the mirror, removing the makeup she applied to conceal the bruises Blotchy had put there a few days prior. Looking at her reflection in disbelief, she patted her wet eyes.

Who would intentionally put someone in jail?

Her mind had been in a frenzy since Myesha played the recording. The voices were unfamiliar, but she was sure her father could decipher the two. She hoped he could.

The clock on her phone read 9:10 pm, and Bobby still hadn't made it home. She wanted to welcome him like a lady, wearing nothing but a robe. Yet, she opted against it. There was no need to steadily entice someone who looked at her through regretful eyes. So, she wore a long-sleeved pajama shirt and pants instead. Jewel went to retrieve a cold glass of milk before heading to bed. Bobby happened to be walking through the door at the same time.

"Hey, you alright?" He was in good spirits.

Jewel's eyes lit up at the sight of the Taco Bell. "Ooohh Taco Bell."

"Yeah. I got you a little something. I figured you'll be hungry. Before I forget, your dad said he loves you and to be on the lookout for his call." He sat the bags on the table and removed his shirt as he headed towards his bedroom.

Jewel sighed deeply. Now she remembered why she had opted out for milk. She flopped down on the sofa. Bobby returned.

"Why you not eating? You didn't have to wait for me." He flopped down next to her and removed his food from the bag.

Without responding, Jewel picked up her phone and played the recording.

At first, Bobby peered at her dumbfounded. His eyes begin to widen. "What the fuck?" He murmured, his mouth full of food. "Fucking bitches," he continued.

"I'm going to tell him about it tomorrow when I go and visit him." Jewel looked as if she had lost all hope. She was sure her father would return home, now this.

"Jewel. Jewel!"

Tears poured down her face. "I miss him so much." She covered her face with her hands, then wailed uncontrollably.

"Ssshhh, stop crying." Bobby wrapped his arms around her, attempting to comfort her.

"He's the only man that has ever loved me."

Bobby let Jewel cry into his chest, until her wails turned into whispers, and all that was left were sniffles here and there. She weakly pulled away.

"Thanks, Bobby. I'm going to bed." She wiped her eyes. "My counselor finally gave me the address to the school. I can go and finish my class. All I need is one more credit."

His brows dipped in confusion. "But tomorrow is Saturday."

"I know." With that, she left him sitting there.

Jewel eased under the covers. The queen size bed was as comfy as her own. However, she longed for Bobby's California king. Reflecting on his muscular arms and toned chest that was exposed after removing his shirt. She moaned in anticipation, as images of their love making flashed through her mind. Everything was so vivid. She could nearly feel it all over again as it replayed.

"Bobby," she whispered. She squirmed underneath the sheets. Her pussy was on fire, and she longed for him to put it out. Not Blotchy, or any other man, she wanted Bobby. She licked her lips as she thought about his rare tool. Even though the tip was a few shades lighter than the shaft, and the rest of his body, she found it quite pleasing. Her mouth watered. She sucked her teeth in hopes of savoring the flavor that was once there, and there it was. Jewel hadn't brushed her teeth since last night. His scent was still there when she lifted her top lip. Even when she swallowed her spit, she could taste him.

Fuck this.

She scurried out of bed. She removed everything she had on, even her frown of frustration. She was headed to take what was

174

hers. Nude as the day she exited her mother's womb, she opened the bedroom door and tip toed into the darkness.

"Ooohh," she squealed. Something hard was blocking her path. *What in the hell?*

She used her hands to feel what she couldn't see.

"Jewel?"

She melted into him at the sound of her name. Unbeknownst to Jewel, her and Bobby were both thinking the same thing. He led her to his bedroom. She gasped at the sight of his nudity. She admired his physique. The dim light from the TV allowed her to see just enough.

Jewel backpedaled to the bed. Her heart beat thunderously in her chest. The bed halted her steps. Bobby hovered over her small frame. He leaned down and covered her mouth with his. They sucked and slurped like they had been waiting on this moment for years.

He lifted her up by the butt cheeks and placed her on the bed. Her ass slightly hung off the edge as she wrapped her legs around Bobby's waist. He pushed her backwards. Jewel squirmed at the feel of his lips on her toes. He sucked each toe, then licked in between them. He planted soft wet kisses from her ankles to the top of her box. He planted kisses from the top of her box to the crack of her ass.

"Open wider."

Jewel did as he requested. Moans filled the room as soon as his warm tongue flickered her button. She almost drew blood she bit her lip so hard.

"Oooh, Bobby," she spoke between panted breaths.

He sucked on her button until she released in his mouth. He eased up. He was now face to face with Jewel. He wanted to love her and love on her forever. But he knew it could never be.

Jewel gasped as Bobby slowly entered her, an inch at a time. He rocked from side to side until he was fully inside of her. She fit him like a glove. Jewel's head fell back, she was in complete bliss. His strokes were sweet and deep, giving her pleasure she didn't know existed. She covered her mouth with her hand, afraid she would burst out into speaking in tongues.

Bobby stood at the edge and pulled her into him. His pace quickened and his strokes shortened. Tears descended Jewel's cheeks in abundance. Bobby's sex had overpowered her senses and lifted her into a trance-like state, a state she wanted to stay in forever.

The next morning, Jewel awoke to an empty bed. Panic set in, but only until the delicious aroma assaulted her nostrils. She jumped out of bed and rummaged through Bobby's drawer. She grabbed the simplest shirt and threw it on.

"Hey," she yelled from the hallway, as soon as she spotted him in the kitchen.

"Good morning," he shot back. He stood over the stove, whipping the eggs.

Damn this nigga look good from every angle, Jewel thought, admiring his back. She stood on the tips of her toes and leaned in for a kiss.

Bobby turned his head to the side and gave her his cheek. Defeated, she sighed deeply and retreated to her room.

"Jewel, come on, man. Where you going?"

Jewel stopped and turned to face him. His constant rejection left her feeling dejected.

"Huh?"

"Where you going?"

She tilted her head back for only a second to cease the tears from falling.

"I'm gon' get ready for school. I have to be there in an hour."

Bobby shrugged. "Cool. I'll sit your plate inside the microwave if you decide to eat."

***

Jewel sat across from her father at the table inside of the visitation area.

"Hey, dad," she said, after giving him a long hug, and then taking her seat.

"I miss you so much, man." Inwardly, Kad wanted to break down, seeing his baby girl.

Jewel's lips started trembling, and then came the tears.

"Come on, Jewel, be strong. Baby, you gonna make a grown man cry." He took a hold of her hands.

"They don't want to see you free, dad."

Kad's brows dipped. "Who, baby girl? Who don't want to see me free?"

Jewel dried her eyes and began informing him on everything she knew.

Ah'Million

Chapter 37
Myesha

The two of them sat in Dooski's car, smoking the potent weed. Jewel was still a little despondent since the visit earlier with her father. She hadn't spoken to Bobby since earlier, before she left for school. He hadn't contacted her either.

"I have to get more cigarillos," Myesha said, pulling out of the lot.

Jewel didn't even protest, she just buckled her seatbelt.

"Bitch, we gon' go splurge at the mall tomorrow, after I get this bag tonight.

"And what are you doing for this bag?"

"One of my fans trying to chill. No sex, we just chillin'."

"Okay I hear you." They pulled up to the smoke shop. Jewel rolled her eyes at all the men who stood around.

"Ugh! Why did we have to come here?"

"I'll only be a second." Myesha strolled inside the store.

Blotchy emerged from the crowd.

"Hey, beautiful." he stood with his hands behind his back, trying to appear innocent.

"Leave me alone, Blotchy." Jewel turned her head.

"Look, I had no business putting my hands on you. Only you can make me so angry because I love you so much. I haven't been the same without you, ma."

Jewel shifted in her seat. She looked at him, then back at the action in front of the store.

"I got something for you. I can wait on your forgiveness but, it deeply bothers me to see you in another nigga shit. Friend or no friend," he voiced, referring to Dooski's ride. He handed her a *Tesla* alarm pad.

She hit the button and the alarm on her new car sounded. She screamed in excitement, seeing the brand-new *Tesla* parked next to her. She looked at Myesha, then back at Blotchy.

Myesha smiled like a proud parent. "Gon' do ya thang. I got to link up with Brandi anyways."

Jewel smacked her lips. "It's cool, you set me up," she voiced, while climbing out the car. "Blotchy, this doesn't mean anything," Jewel continued, hopping inside the Tesla.

"It's yours, no strings attached. Hit me up whenever you ready." Neither of them believed that. "You know where I'm at." He smirked.

Jewel and Myesha burnt off simultaneously.

***

"I don't know about this." Myesha peaked out of the restroom door into the suite, where everyone else waited.

"It's cool, baby sis." Brandi twirled in a circle, snapping her fingers.

Brandi made Myesha's body look average, compared to her curvaceous figure. Myesha rubbed her arm, while listening to Brandi.

Brandi grabbed Myesha by the shoulders. "Look, you don't have to dance. These dudes just paid us to chill."

"Me?" she pointed to herself. "I'm trying to get knee deep in their pockets, so I'm gon' throw a lil' ass so they can throw a lil' cash. Bitch, that's Dusse on top of Dusse on the table."

Myesha looked at her dumbfounded.

"Lawd, you don't even know what Dusse is. Just know they got some cash. Come on." She led Myesha out of the restroom by the hand. She bopped through the suite, making her D cup, perky breasts jump in the neon pink bikini top.

Shawty smokin' zaza out the pack, I told her roll up.
Niggas muggin' stupid, lookin' crazy, like they know us.
You ain't got no money, plus you bummy and you tore up.
You pretty, but bitch so what? (Hd)
Me and Bossie in the Maybach, good and full of liquor.
Seen a cutie with a booty, tryna jugg her with this pickle.
All my niggas rollin' backwoods. They don't fuck around with swishers.
I been fuckin' on his bitch, I was just fuckin on her sister.

"Uh uh, Brandi," Myesha jerked her hand from her sister's grasp.

"Zya!"

Zya peered through the semi-packed crowd and instantly spotted her friend. She hopped off the guy's lap she was entertaining and rushed to her aid.

"What's up, bitch? Where you been?" She slurred.

Brandi sighed deeply. "Watch my lil' sister real quick. She on the edge and I need to get her right." Brandi winked at Zya.

"Oh, bitch, I got so-" Zya was reaching inside of her breast when Brandi grabbed her arm.

"Nah, not that." She wagged her finger. "She's a beginner." Brandi turned and looked at Myesha. "Give me a hug." She squeezed her tight.

"I'll be back. Let me grab my phone." Brandi vanished.

Myesha stood there next to Zya, unsure of what to do next.

"Come on, I'm 'bout to put you on these bread winna's."

Ah'Million

Chapter 38
Brandi

"Hey Dooski, is Myesha here?"

He scowled. "I don't know where she at. I can't even go look for her 'cause she in my shit." Veins protruded from his neck.

"Look!" Brandi, held up her hands. "I'm on my way to work and I stopped by to borrow some jewelry, but since she's not here, let me pee and I'll be on my way."

Dooski moved to the side, allowing Brandi inside. Her ass hung out of the neon pink latex boy shorts. He lowered his head.

You tripping man. That's her sister.

He slammed the door shut, then sighed deeply before flopping on the couch. He fidgeted with the hairs on his chin, as he thought about the whereabouts of his chick. Brandi emerged from the restroom, using her long freshly manicured nails to adjust the front of her shorts. She looked like a whole meal and dessert. Fuck a *snack.* She cupped her breast as if she was looking for something.

"Oh, I left it in the car," she stated aloud. "Shit." She dropped her keys with her backside towards Dooski. She bent over slowly and picked them up. With her ass still toward him, she used her index finger to slowly pull her bottoms out of her ass.

Dooski wanted to bend her over the arm of the sofa. Yet, he just couldn't bring himself to do it. She strutted towards the door.

"If I talk to her before you do, I'll let her know you looking for her."

Ah'Million

Chapter 39
Blotchy

Number two

Blotchy had counted mentally how many times in the same day he heard the same thing. The dude he beat down in his store weeks ago was steady poppin' his hit. He caressed the hair on his chin, while staring aimlessly out the window.

"I'm not worried 'bout dude. The same place I got at 'em is the same place he can find me."

The guy that delivered the message nodded his head and proceeded to the back of the store, where the dice game was held.

Blotchy had been expecting a call from Bobby so that they could link up and record his final song for the album. Since hooking up with Bobby and Kad, Dooski had been begging him for a feature, but he kindly declined because he was too busy solidifying his spot. He didn't have time to be concerned about someone else's music, no matter who it was. Both of them were lyrically talented. However, they possessed a different style of music. Blotchy hadn't spoken to Dooski much since the mishap. He made a mental note to call him later.

"Blotchy." The guy smirked. "Check this ho out, she puttin' on for her city." He showed Blotchy his phone.

Blotchy's brows dipped. It was Myesha.

"And lil mama got a *Only Fans*," he continued his praise.

"How you know she got a *Only Fans*?" Blotchy leaned in inquisitively.

"It says it right there." He pointed to the screen.

Blotchy nodded silently but chuckled inwardly.

Dumb ass think he lucked up and found a pot of gold. Should've took it to the jeweler before staking claim 'cause the only thing inside of that pot is a bunch of costume jewelry.

"Shoot me the video and let's check out her *Only Fans*. Lil' mama do look like a *snack*."

Indeed, Myesha looked good, but he was really just gassin' to get dude to expose everything there was about Myesha.

He peered back at Blotchy, uncertainty in his eyes.

"Whats up?"

"Big homie, it's a *hundred* dollars to look at her *Only Fans*." Blotchy didn't give a damn 'bout the shame that laced his words.

"Damn, lil' nigga, you ain't got a hunnid dollars?"

"Yeah, to fuck some pussy, but not to look at any, especially if I can't touch it." He shrugged.

"That's real." Blotchy reached into his pocket and retrieved his cash app card. "Here."

Ring. Ring. Ring.

"Hello?"

"This Blotchy?"

His face scrunched as he tried to decipher the voice. "Yeah, who wants to know?"

"Calm down, youngsta. This Todd with MGM, Rozay wants to fly you out to *ATL* and offer you a deal you won't refuse."

Blotchy hid his excitement, not wanting to sound eager or thirsty. "Oh, that sounds good. When?"

"Tomorrow."

"Tomorrow?" He looked down at his apple watch. "Look, today is Tuesday. Is Thursday cool? I run my own business and I got to make sure things straight before I leave."

"That's fine. I'll text you the details. Peace."

"Hell yeah," Blotchy mumbled. He couldn't wait to tell Dooski. He shot a text to Bobby, something he had wanted to do days ago because he felt like their label was full of shit.

Blotchy: *Aye, I'm out. Found some better.*

"Here, big homie," the young guy said, handing Blotchy the phone.

Blotchy could've told Dooski, but he thought of a better idea. He would use Myesha to get Dooski and Jewel back, together. Instantly, he facetimed Myesha.

"Blotchy?" She asked, peering confusingly into the screen.

Blotchy held up the guy's phone, swiping the screen slowly through her *Only Fans* gallery. Shame coupled with anger, as she lowered her head.

"You don't got to look like that." He paused, smirking menacingly. "All you have to do is talk some sense into your homegirl, and you'll never hear a peep out of me."

Ah'Million

It's Just Me and You

Chapter 40
Bobby

"What's up, boy," Kad asked.

"Pulling away from my big mama house."

"Next time you go over there, tell her hey and I love her."

"Bet." Bobby fixed his eyes on the road.

"Aye, another thing, drop Blotchy."

"Let him go scot-free?" Bobby inquired.

"Yep. He don't have to pay anything to get out of the contract. That's how much I want him gone."

Bobby smirked. "Bet."

Bobby had to handle some things at the office before going home. He was pleased with Kad's decision. He was leery of Bobby from the jump.

The lot was pretty empty, three to four cars were scattered here and there. Bobby and Kad shared the space with a *Cricket* and a *Jackson Hewitt*. He needed to do his homework on the next investor. The meeting with Ms. Combs was just two days away. He jogged up to the front of the office. As he inserted his keys into the door, he heard his name. He peered back and saw Sierra rushing in his direction. Her heels clacking with each step.

Bobby sighed deeply. He thought Kad would tell her the real, instead of him having to do it, even though he had no problem doing so. Since meeting Sierra, he disliked her. Her flirty eyes and promiscuous spirit annoyed him. Pure disrespect to his friend. And if he was the typical dude, he would have been smashed. She held no loyalty. *Then and now.* She was only there for Kad now so she could secure a spot back in his life, business, and finances, upon his release, or perhaps now, Bobby thought.

It wasn't going to happen on his watch.

"Hey." She panted, removing the strands out of her face.

"What's up?" He glared at her through uninviting eyes.

"Kat told-"

He held up his hand, ceasing her speech. "I already told Kad, while he's gone, I got this. I don't need no help. But I appreciate you for-"

She held her finger to Bobby's lips. He slapped her hand down, while glaring at her in bewilderment.

"Oooh." She jerked back, afraid he would hit her. "Look, Bobby." She took a step backwards. "Get with the program or I'll tell your boy." She held up quotation signs with her hands. "That you sticking dick to his seventeen year old daughter."

How in the hell?

Baffled, he blinked a few times. He felt like she had taken a knife and plunged him in the heart, twisted it, then pulled it back out. What he thought was a secret, between him and Jewel, had been exposed. The toughest man nor circumstances had ever made Bobby tuck his tail. However, here he was submitting to the hands of a woman.

***

"Jewel!" He called out, entering his home.

"Huh?" She darted from the back.

"Who car is that in the driveway?"

"Oh," she paused, stepping closer. "A friend bought it for me."

Jealousy surged through Bobby instantly, but he tried his best to hide it. "Cool, make sure you tell your dad." He walked past her, leaving her standing there.

Bobby was furious. He knew her friend was a guy, and niggas were not buying cars for the hell of it.

She's fucking someone else.

"I missed you." She rocked on the ball of her feet.

"I don't want to hear none of that." He left the kitchen and went inside his bedroom. He slammed his door and locked it.

Chapter 41
Jewel

Tears silently rolled down Jewel's cheeks. She had never witnessed Bobby so raw and uncut. If the rejection wasn't enough, this surely was. Her and Blotchy had been texting back and forth for the past thirty minutes. However, she had yet to respond to his last text.

Blotchy: *I want to C you.*

She turned her phone face down and laid it on top of the covers. There was no denying the fact that she did miss Blotchy, but the grip Bobby had on her was deadly. Like she had done last night and the night before last, she undressed and tip-toed to his bedroom. She slowly twisted the knob on the door.

It was locked.

A wave of dejection and anger consumed her. She strutted back to her bedroom and got dressed, completely dressed.

Jewel: *Drop your location.*

She threw her hair in a messy bun and hopped in her Tesla.

Jewel had never seen the inside of Blotchy's place.

Power of that P, get a nigga right.

She smirked. Just a pair of Ralph Lauren briefs and matching pajamas pants. Jewel couldn't help but stare at his chiseled abdomen, covered in professional tattoos.

Down girl.

You want something to eat?

"Nah, it's too late." Jewel looked around. She was pleased with his taste. Blotchy came and sat on the sofa next to her. They sat and talked for hours, until Jewel finally called it a night.

On the ride back to Bobby's, she re-evaluated everything Blotchy had said. She wanted to believe every word that fell from his lips, but it had been proven that he could not be trusted. She sighed deeply before exiting her vehicle. It had been a long night. She unlocked the door and felt around for the light switch. She found the switch and an angry Bobby sitting in the love seat.

"Bobby," she whispered, grabbing her chest.

"Save that shit. You can't come and go whenever you please. It's rules here, too. Since you can't respect that," he stood and walked towards her, "Here."

Jewel looked at the money, dumbfounded.

"Go get you a room. You can't stay here."

She was appalled. "Really, Bobby? A damn curfew?" She screamed.

Little did she know, a curfew was his least concern.

"You damn right!" He shot back.

Tears blurred her vision as she brushed past him to collect her things. Mostly everything was still in bags, the way she had brought it. So, it took her no time. After placing all her bags in the car, she walked up to Bobby, who was leaned against the counter.

Emotion coupled with distress, she spoke through clenched teeth. "You wouldn't have to worry about if I'm out there giving another nigga what yours, if only you'd act like it's yours for motherfucking once."

Bobby smacked his lips.

Jewel darted for the door.

Chapter 42
Myesha

Myesha sat in the passenger seat of her sister's car. Brandi was inside of the beauty supply house, picking up a few items.

Ring. Ring.

Myesha snapped her head in the direction of the ringing phone that sat in the cup holder.

Mama?

Myesha declined the call, then deleted it from Brandi's call history.

"My bad, girl, I almost had to curse that damn chink out," Brandi rambled, climbing inside the car. "So, have you thought about it?" She asked, pulling away from the store.

"Yes, and I'm not going." Myesha paused. "I don't think Dooski believes I was with Jewel that night. He gives me this ol' suspect ass look every time it comes up."

Brandi waved her hand. "Girl, that ain't shit. It's gon' be a whole lot of money in that motherfucka."

Myesha's brow raised. "More money than last time?" She had made close to five g's. Now that she had a taste of fast money, she was hooked.

Brandi slowly shook her head. A mischievous smile decorated her face.

"Count me in."

"Hell yeah, let's go fuck up some commas."

"Brandi." Myesha paused.

"Sup?"

"Have you talked to mama?"

Brandi looked at Myesha like she had two heads. "Hell nah, I don't even have her number saved in my phone. I don't fuck with her."

"Ok." Myesha nodded slowly, confused as to why her sister would bluntly lie to her.

"Why you ask that?"

"Well, I asked cause-"

Ring. Ring. Ring.

"Hold on," Myesha said, getting her phone out of her purse. It was Dooski.

"Hey, baby," she answered coolly.

"Bae, some niggas just shot up Blotchy's car! Jewel was in there! We up here at Bayor, hurry up!"

To Be Continued...
It's Just Me and You 2
Coming Soon

Lock Down Publications and Ca$h Presents assisted publishing packages.

BASIC PACKAGE $499
Editing
Cover Design
Formatting

UPGRADED PACKAGE $800
Typing
Editing
Cover Design
Formatting

ADVANCE PACKAGE $1,200
Typing
Editing
Cover Design
Formatting
Copyright registration
Proofreading
Upload book to Amazon

LDP SUPREME PACKAGE $1,500
Typing
Editing
Cover Design
Formatting
Copyright registration
Proofreading
Set up Amazon account
Upload book to Amazon
Advertise on LDP Amazon and Facebook page

***Other services available upon request. Additional charges may apply
Lock Down Publications
P.O. Box 944
Stockbridge, GA 30281-9998
Phone # 470 303-9761

Submission Guideline

Submit the first three chapters of your completed manuscript to ldpsubmissions@gmail.com, subject line: Your book's title. The manuscript must be in a .doc file and sent as an attachment. Document should be in Times New Roman, double spaced and in size 12 font. Also, provide your synopsis and full contact information. If sending multiple submissions, they must each be in a separate email.

Have a story but no way to send it electronically? You can still submit to LDP/Ca$h Presents. Send in the first three chapters, written or typed, of your completed manuscript to:

LDP: Submissions Dept
Po Box 944
Stockbridge, Ga 30281

DO NOT send original manuscript. Must be a duplicate.

Provide your synopsis and a cover letter containing your full contact information.

Thanks for considering LDP and Ca$h Presents.

<u>NEW RELEASES</u>

PROTÉGÉ OF A LEGEND by COREY ROBINSON
STRAIGHT BEAST MODE 2 by DE'KARI
ANGEL 3 by ANTHONY FIELDS
CLASSIC CITY by CHRIS GREEN
TIL DEATH by ARYANNA
IT'S JUST ME AND YOU by AH'MILLION

STRAIGHT BEAST MODE III

De'Kari

KINGPIN KILLAZ IV

STREET KINGS III

PAID IN BLOOD III

CARTEL KILLAZ IV

DOPE GODS III

Hood Rich

SINS OF A HUSTLA II

ASAD

RICH $AVAGE II

By Martell Troublesome Bolden

YAYO V

Bred In The Game 2

S. Allen

CREAM III

THE STREETS WILL TALK II

By Yolanda Moore

SON OF A DOPE FIEND III

HEAVEN GOT A GHETTO II

By Renta

LOYALTY AIN'T PROMISED III

By Keith Williams

I'M NOTHING WITHOUT HIS LOVE II

SINS OF A THUG II

TO THE THUG I LOVED BEFORE II

IN A HUSTLER I TRUST II

By Monet Dragun

QUIET MONEY IV

EXTENDED CLIP III

THUG LIFE IV

By **Trai'Quan**

THE STREETS MADE ME IV

By **Larry D. Wright**

IF YOU CROSS ME ONCE II

ANGEL IV

By **Anthony Fields**

THE STREETS WILL NEVER CLOSE IV

By **K'ajji**

HARD AND RUTHLESS III

KILLA KOUNTY III

By **Khufu**

MONEY GAME III

By **Smoove Dolla**

JACK BOYS VS DOPE BOYS II

A GANGSTA'S QUR'AN V

COKE GIRLZ II

By **Romell Tukes**

MURDA WAS THE CASE II

Elijah R. Freeman

THE STREETS NEVER LET GO II

By **Robert Baptiste**

AN UNFORESEEN LOVE III

By **Meesha**

KING OF THE TRENCHES III

by **GHOST & TRANAY ADAMS**

MONEY MAFIA II

LOYAL TO THE SOIL III

By **Jibril Williams**

QUEEN OF THE ZOO II

By **Black Migo**
VICIOUS LOYALTY III
By Kingpen
A GANGSTA'S PAIN III
By J-Blunt
CONFESSIONS OF A JACKBOY III
By Nicholas Lock
GRIMEY WAYS II
By Ray Vinci
KING KILLA II
By Vincent "Vitto" Holloway
BETRAYAL OF A THUG II
By Fre$h
THE MURDER QUEENS II
By Michael Gallon
THE BIRTH OF A GANGSTER II
By Delmont Player
TREAL LOVE II
By Le'Monica Jackson
FOR THE LOVE OF BLOOD II
By Jamel Mitchell
RAN OFF ON DA PLUG II
By Paper Boi Rari
HOOD CONSIGLIERE II
By Keese
PRETTY GIRLS DO NASTY THINGS II
By Nicole Goosby
PROTÉGÉ OF A LEGEND II
By Corey Robinson
IT'S JUST ME AND YOU II

Ah'Million

By Ah'Million

BLOODY COMMAS I & II

SKI MASK CARTEL I II & III

KING OF NEW YORK I II,III IV V

RISE TO POWER I II III

COKE KINGS I II III IV V

BORN HEARTLESS I II III IV

KING OF THE TRAP I II

By **T.J. Edwards**

IF LOVING HIM IS WRONG…I & II

LOVE ME EVEN WHEN IT HURTS I II III

By **Jelissa**

WHEN THE STREETS CLAP BACK I & II III

THE HEART OF A SAVAGE I II III

MONEY MAFIA

LOYAL TO THE SOIL I II

By **Jibril Williams**

A DISTINGUISHED THUG STOLE MY HEART I II & III

LOVE SHOULDN'T HURT I II III IV

RENEGADE BOYS I II III IV

PAID IN KARMA I II III

SAVAGE STORMS I II III

AN UNFORESEEN LOVE I II

By **Meesha**

A GANGSTER'S CODE I &, II III

A GANGSTER'S SYN I II III

THE SAVAGE LIFE I II III

CHAINED TO THE STREETS I II III

BLOOD ON THE MONEY I II III

A GANGSTA'S PAIN I II

By **J-Blunt**

Ah'Million

PUSH IT TO THE LIMIT

By **Bre' Hayes**

BLOOD OF A BOSS **I, II, III, IV, V**

SHADOWS OF THE GAME

TRAP BASTARD

By **Askari**

THE STREETS BLEED MURDER **I, II & III**

THE HEART OF A GANGSTA I II& III

By **Jerry Jackson**

CUM FOR ME I II III IV V VI VII VIII

An **LDP Erotica Collaboration**

BRIDE OF A HUSTLA **I II & II**

THE FETTI GIRLS **I, II& III**

CORRUPTED BY A GANGSTA I, II III, IV

BLINDED BY HIS LOVE

THE PRICE YOU PAY FOR LOVE I, II ,III

DOPE GIRL MAGIC I II III

By **Destiny Skai**

WHEN A GOOD GIRL GOES BAD

By **Adrienne**

THE COST OF LOYALTY I II III

By Kweli

A GANGSTER'S REVENGE **I II III & IV**

THE BOSS MAN'S DAUGHTERS I II III IV V

A SAVAGE LOVE **I & II**

BAE BELONGS TO ME I II

A HUSTLER'S DECEIT I, II, III

WHAT BAD BITCHES DO I, II, III

SOUL OF A MONSTER I II III

KILL ZONE

It's Just Me and You

A DOPE BOY'S QUEEN I II III

TIL DEATH

By **Aryanna**

A KINGPIN'S AMBITON

A KINGPIN'S AMBITION **II**

I MURDER FOR THE DOUGH

By **Ambitious**

TRUE SAVAGE I II III IV V VI VII

DOPE BOY MAGIC I, II, III

MIDNIGHT CARTEL I II III

CITY OF KINGZ I II

NIGHTMARE ON SILENT AVE

THE PLUG OF LIL MEXICO II

CLASSIC CITY

By **Chris Green**

A DOPEBOY'S PRAYER

By **Eddie "Wolf" Lee**

THE KING CARTEL **I, II & III**

By **Frank Gresham**

THESE NIGGAS AIN'T LOYAL **I, II & III**

By **Nikki Tee**

GANGSTA SHYT **I II &III**

By **CATO**

THE ULTIMATE BETRAYAL

By **Phoenix**

BOSS'N UP **I , II & III**

By **Royal Nicole**

I LOVE YOU TO DEATH

By **Destiny J**

I RIDE FOR MY HITTA

I STILL RIDE FOR MY HITTA

By **Misty Holt**

LOVE & CHASIN' PAPER

By **Qay Crockett**

TO DIE IN VAIN

SINS OF A HUSTLA

By **ASAD**

BROOKLYN HUSTLAZ

By **Boogsy Morina**

BROOKLYN ON LOCK I & II

By **Sonovia**

GANGSTA CITY

By **Teddy Duke**

A DRUG KING AND HIS DIAMOND I & II III

A DOPEMAN'S RICHES

HER MAN, MINE'S TOO I, II

CASH MONEY HO'S

THE WIFEY I USED TO BE I II

PRETTY GIRLS DO NASTY THINGS

By Nicole Goosby

TRAPHOUSE KING **I II & III**

KINGPIN KILLAZ I II III

STREET KINGS I II

PAID IN BLOOD **I II**

CARTEL KILLAZ I II III

DOPE GODS I II

By **Hood Rich**

LIPSTICK KILLAH **I, II, III**

CRIME OF PASSION I II & III

FRIEND OR FOE I II III

It's Just Me and You

By **Mimi**

STEADY MOBBN' **I, II, III**

THE STREETS STAINED MY SOUL I II III

By **Marcellus Allen**

WHO SHOT YA **I, II, III**

SON OF A DOPE FIEND I II

HEAVEN GOT A GHETTO

Renta

GORILLAZ IN THE BAY **I II III IV**

TEARS OF A GANGSTA I II

3X KRAZY I II

STRAIGHT BEAST MODE I II

DE'KARI

TRIGGADALE I II III

MURDAROBER WAS THE CASE

Elijah R. Freeman

GOD BLESS THE TRAPPERS I, II, III

THESE SCANDALOUS STREETS I, II, III

FEAR MY GANGSTA I, II, III IV, V

THESE STREETS DON'T LOVE NOBODY I, II

BURY ME A G I, II, III, IV, V

A GANGSTA'S EMPIRE I, II, III, IV

THE DOPEMAN'S BODYGAURD I II

THE REALEST KILLAZ I II III

THE LAST OF THE OGS I II III

Tranay Adams

THE STREETS ARE CALLING

Duquie Wilson

MARRIED TO A BOSS I II III

By Destiny Skai & Chris Green

Ah'Million

KINGZ OF THE GAME I II III IV V VI
Playa Ray
SLAUGHTER GANG I II III
RUTHLESS HEART I II III
By Willie Slaughter
FUK SHYT
By Blakk Diamond
DON'T F#CK WITH MY HEART I II
By Linnea
ADDICTED TO THE DRAMA I II III
IN THE ARM OF HIS BOSS II
By Jamila
YAYO I II III IV
A SHOOTER'S AMBITION I II
BRED IN THE GAME
By S. Allen
TRAP GOD I II III
RICH $AVAGE
MONEY IN THE GRAVE I II III
By Martell Troublesome Bolden
FOREVER GANGSTA
GLOCKS ON SATIN SHEETS I II
By Adrian Dulan
TOE TAGZ I II III IV
LEVELS TO THIS SHYT I II
IT'S JUST ME AND YOU
By Ah'Million
KINGPIN DREAMS I II III
RAN OFF ON DA PLUG
By Paper Boi Rari

208

It's Just Me and You

CONFESSIONS OF A GANGSTA I II III IV

CONFESSIONS OF A JACKBOY I II

By Nicholas Lock

I'M NOTHING WITHOUT HIS LOVE

SINS OF A THUG

TO THE THUG I LOVED BEFORE

A GANGSTA SAVED XMAS

IN A HUSTLER I TRUST

By Monet Dragun

CAUGHT UP IN THE LIFE I II III

THE STREETS NEVER LET GO

By Robert Baptiste

NEW TO THE GAME I II III

MONEY, MURDER & MEMORIES I II III

By **Malik D. Rice**

LIFE OF A SAVAGE I II III

A GANGSTA'S QUR'AN I II III IV

MURDA SEASON I II III

GANGLAND CARTEL I II III

CHI'RAQ GANGSTAS I II III

KILLERS ON ELM STREET I II III

JACK BOYZ N DA BRONX I II III

A DOPEBOY'S DREAM I II III

JACK BOYS VS DOPE BOYS

COKE GIRLZ

By Romell Tukes

LOYALTY AIN'T PROMISED I II

By Keith Williams

QUIET MONEY I II III

THUG LIFE I II III

Ah'Million

EXTENDED CLIP I II

By **Trai'Quan**

THE STREETS MADE ME I II III

By **Larry D. Wright**

THE ULTIMATE SACRIFICE I, II, III, IV, V, VI

KHADIFI

IF YOU CROSS ME ONCE

ANGEL I II III

IN THE BLINK OF AN EYE

By **Anthony Fields**

THE LIFE OF A HOOD STAR

By Ca$h & Rashia Wilson

THE STREETS WILL NEVER CLOSE I II III

By K'ajji

CREAM I II

THE STREETS WILL TALK

By Yolanda Moore

NIGHTMARES OF A HUSTLA I II III

By King Dream

CONCRETE KILLA I II III

VICIOUS LOYALTY I II

By Kingpen

HARD AND RUTHLESS I II

MOB TOWN 251

THE BILLIONAIRE BENTLEYS I II III

By Von Diesel

GHOST MOB

Stilloan Robinson

MOB TIES I II III IV V VI

By SayNoMore

BODYMORE MURDERLAND I II III
THE BIRTH OF A GANGSTER
By Delmont Player
FOR THE LOVE OF A BOSS
By C. D. Blue
MOBBED UP I II III IV
THE BRICK MAN I II III IV
THE COCAINE PRINCESS I II III IV V
By King Rio
KILLA KOUNTY I II III
By Khufu
MONEY GAME I II
By Smoove Dolla
A GANGSTA'S KARMA I II
By FLAME
KING OF THE TRENCHES I II
by **GHOST & TRANAY ADAMS**
QUEEN OF THE ZOO
By **Black Migo**
GRIMEY WAYS
By Ray Vinci
XMAS WITH AN ATL SHOOTER
By Ca$h & Destiny Skai
KING KILLA
By Vincent "Vitto" Holloway
BETRAYAL OF A THUG
By Fre$h
THE MURDER QUEENS
By Michael Gallon
TREAL LOVE

Ah'Million

By Le'Monica Jackson
FOR THE LOVE OF BLOOD
By Jamel Mitchell
HOOD CONSIGLIERE
By Keese
PROTÉGÉ OF A LEGEND
By Corey Robinson

BOOKS BY LDP'S CEO, CA$H

TRUST IN NO MAN

TRUST IN NO MAN 2

TRUST IN NO MAN 3

BONDED BY BLOOD

SHORTY GOT A THUG

THUGS CRY

THUGS CRY 2

THUGS CRY 3

TRUST NO BITCH

TRUST NO BITCH 2

TRUST NO BITCH 3

TIL MY CASKET DROPS

RESTRAINING ORDER

RESTRAINING ORDER 2

IN LOVE WITH A CONVICT

LIFE OF A HOOD STAR

XMAS WITH AN ATL SHOOTER

Ah'Million